ROO

Carter
the per...

Her naked body was stretched across the bed, legs spread in an erotic pose. Carter snapped the lock on the door and started edging toward the closet.

"You very big man. I like big man. Come to bed with Sim Li, I give you good time all night."

Carter yanked open the closed door. His bag was gone. Behind him, he heard Sim Li's feet hit the floor. He lunged, hitting her hip-high and sending her sailing against the far wall.

The stiletto flashed in the Killmaster's right hand.

She came at him, her left hand extended, palm up and fingers stiff, her right hand pulled back alongside her head, ready to strike. He spun as he ducked, and the outside edge of his right boot caught her just above the left elbow. Still pivoting, he brought his right hand down and caught her with the hardened edge just below the skull on her pretty neck. She landed on her side and slid to a stop just short of the door.

"Try that again," the Killmaster growled, "and I'll use the blade."

NICK CARTER IS IT!

FROM THE NICK CARTER
KILLMASTER SERIES

THE RANGOON MAN

KILL MASTER

NICK CARTER

JOVE BOOKS, NEW YORK

KILLMASTER #240: THE RANGOON MAN

A Jove Book / published by arrangement with
The Condé Nast Publications, Inc.

PRINTING HISTORY
Jove editon / August 1988

ISBN: 0-515-09681-4

Jove Books are published by The Berkley Publishing Group.
200 Madison Avenue, New York, New York 10016.
The name "JOVE" and the "J" logo
are trademarks belonging to Jove Publications, Inc.

PRINTED IN THE UNITED STATES OF AMERICA

10 9 8 7 6 5 4 3 2 1

Dedicated to the men of the
Secret Services of the
United States of America

THE RANGOON MAN

ONE

The noise of the windshield wipers made a steady *flip-flap* sound. It had been only a sprinkle through the Three Pagodas Pass, but now, as the road swung toward the Gulf of Martaban, it was coming down in thick, blinding sheets.

Between Bangkok and the pass, he had been forced to stay much closer to the six-truck caravan. But now, thankfully, he could let them roll ahead. There was only one road up the coast and around to Rangoon, so he had to pick them up again eventually.

Charles Verrain raised one hand from the wheel to rub his eyes. They ached from peering into the night through the rain. The hand then dipped into one of the two loaded and bulky camera bags beside him and fumbled until he found a cigarette. He lit it and inhaled deeply.

The gas station attendant who had filled the Land-Rover that morning had warned him that it wasn't just a light morning rain. It was the tongue of the first monsoon of the season. It would last, it would grow heavier, the roads would be bad, and there would probably be washout.

He really shouldn't travel.

But if the trucks traveled, he would have to travel. He

1

had plied his trade of photojournalism in the Thai hills across the frontier from the Cambodian village of Paoy Pet for days, waiting for the shipment to be slipped over and loaded onto the trucks.

"It has to be Paoy Pet," the analyzers in Washington had said. "They must bring them out of Vietnam and transport them across the northern part of Cambodia. It's ten to one they're trucked from there. What we need to know is where they go, and verification of the quality and quantity."

After four days of watching, Verrain had begun to think Washington was full of beans. But then one morning the trucks came, and that night the crates came over and were loaded.

And Verrain had followed them. It had rained all day, heavily since noon and the crossover into Burma. The Land-Rover that the MI6 people had provided was unreliable. It pulled badly on the hills, and had enough fits of coughing and missing that several times Verrain thought he would have to abort the mission or steal some other transportation.

He rubbed his eyes again. It was difficult to see the road. Now and again he picked out the white gleam of painted posts, but it was easier to hug the black fringe of boulders on the road's inner side. The road tilted and a wide frothy torrent of rainwater continually swept downward. When the wheels dropped into a filled pothole, a great fan of spray was flung backward at the windshield.

By now Verrain figured he was almost down from the hills. According to the map, there should be only a few kilometers left before the next village, Kamwaddy. With any luck the trucks would stop there for gas, maybe even shelter if the storm got any worse.

And with a little more luck maybe he could get a look inside, at the crates and their contents.

Suddenly the mini-river running along the inner side of

the road swung away from the black line of boulders and drew a white line of foam across the road.

Verrain braked the car and stopped, the back wheels skidding as they bit against the mud. He stared through the windshield. Under the rain-broken lights, the road showed rough, distorted, and heaped with rock.

Cursing, he reached for his flashlight in the door pocket and got out. The wind ripped at his raincoat, shaking its tails, and the hard rain played a tattoo on his face as he bent against the storm. He moved forward cautiously, his flashlight trained on the ground ahead of him.

"Shit," he muttered aloud.

Slide, and partial washout.

It looked as if it had just happened. Smaller rocks and dirt were still coming down the hill. There was no room to get the Land-Rover around, and even if there were, he didn't think the road would take the weight.

Swearing under his breath, he moved back to the Rover. There was nothing he could do; he would have to walk to Kamwaddy. He pulled the two camera bags from the seat and slung them over his shoulders. From the rear he got his small travel bag and set off.

He moved off the road and circled the pile of dirt and rocks. To his left, over the sea, a bright flame of lightning flickered. For an instant he thought he saw buildings in its illumination.

He walked, and in less than a mile his shoes were full of cold, uncomfortable water. A tunnel of rain worked itself under his collar and ran down his back. Discomfort spread over his shoulders when the heavy camera-bag straps cut into them.

He was suddenly aware that he was cursing aloud, cursing the rain and David Hawk and AXE who had put him out in the middle of all this.

Then he rounded a curve and saw where the road had again washed out. There was a four-foot crater where it had been, and in the crater was a truck. Its front wheel and cab had dropped over the edge of the broken road. It rested on a pile of rock, and the entire body of the vehicle was tilted at a crazy angle.

Verrain moved closer to examine it. He saw at once what had happened. It had come up the road and dropped gently with its front wheels into the shallow edge of the crater.

It was one of theirs. It must have been the rear truck. The others had gotten through, and the last man must have been caught by the sudden washout. He had evidently abandoned the truck and run on to find his fellows.

Verrain dropped his travel bag and slopped through the mud until he was at the truck bed. The body had tilted, and through the rotted canvas canopy two or three wooden cases had cracked open, springing their lids.

Luck, he thought, *my God, what luck!*

Gingerly, he hauled himself up into the rear of the truck and examined them. Stenciled on the top and sides of each crate were the words SYDNEY CHONG, IMPORT/EXPORT, FINE ANTIQUES, RANGOON.

With his light he examined the interior of the three open crates. They were heavily matted with packing straw, and in the straw he found small statues, framed paintings, and velvet boxes containing carved jade.

Did he dare rip open the other crates? If he had to, he would. But in the meantime . . . .

He dug further into the straw, and minutes later found what Washington had guessed would be there.

Two of the crates contained heavy canisters of napalm. In the bottom of the third crate he found Stinger surface-to-air missiles. All of them were stamped PROPERTY U.S. GOVERNMENT.

Verrain counted the crates. There were sixty-five of them. Sixty-five crates times six trucks added up to the start of a nice little war.

He dug out his infrared camera and started snapping away.

He had nearly finished a whole roll when, far in the distance, he heard the growl of a truck engine.

They were coming back, probably to transfer this load to an empty vehicle.

Quickly, Verrain replaced the straw and the lids as he had found them. He jumped from the truck, scrambled out of the crater, and retrieved his travel bag. He ran back down the road about thirty yards and then began climbing up the side of the hill. He had barely ducked behind some large rocks when a pair of headlights broke over the hill coming from the direction of Kamwaddy.

The other truck came slowly up the long slope and stopped at the wrecked one. He heard the shout of men's voices. He saw four forms stir across the headlights and then one man stood for a while in the full blaze. His figure was picked out in a radiance of wet reflections . . . tall, bald-headed, the collar of an old raincoat turned up around his neck.

Verrain could see the face clearly. It was a long, cruel face, brown skin, small nose, almond-shaped dark eyes.

Suddenly the man barked orders and the four of them began transferring the crates.

Verrain eased his breath out and hunkered down. He would wait until they were gone.

By the time he reached the outskirts of Kamwaddy, his shoes were sodden masses of leather, and his trousers and the bottom of his raincoat were caked with heavy mud.

Even though the hour was very late, there were still dim lights on in many of the buildings. Two blocks away he saw a sign in Burmese characters: a hotel.

Only steps away was an outdoor stall with five stools. Under the flopping, leaky canvas covering, an ancient Burmese woman cooked curry and rice, unmindful of the wind and rain.

Verrain darted in and sat. He ordered a plate of food. The old woman set it and tea before him and returned to her pots, as oblivious of him as she was of the torrent outside.

He rewound the film and flipped it from the camera. Then he took two envelopes from the bottom of the bag. On one he wrote, *Leonard Markham, Consulate General of U.S., 170 Strand Road, Rangoon, Burma*. On the other he wrote, *Eyes Only—Richard Garfield, Amalgamated Press, Hong Kong—To Be Pouch Delivered*.

The film went into the second envelope and it into the first. Practically all mail leaving Burma was censored. By sending it this way, Verrain knew it would reach Markham and be delivered on to Hong Kong without any disruption.

He paid for his meal and walked on up the street to the hotel. Just inside the first door there was a mailbox. He dropped the letter in and pushed open the second door.

Just inside he paused, narrowing his eyes to see in the hard light. Like all cheap native hotels in Burma, the lobby served as all-purpose registration area, bar, restaurant, and general lounge. This one was no different. There were stairs to his left, tables to his right, and a bar in front of him. It was wood-topped and pyramided with glasses and bottles. At one end was a small glass case with cigars and a few packs of local cigarettes.

At the end of the bar, a diminutive man wearing the traditional Burmese sarong skirt, the cotton *xongui*, sat at a battered piano fiddling with the keys. A glass of rice wine was near his fingers and a cigarette hung from the corner of his mouth.

As Verrain walked forward, his nostrils were assaulted with the odors of fish, stale beer, and wet clothing. He dropped his bag, sat, and froze.

They were there, the five truck drivers. The table where they sat had been blocked from his view when he came through the door.

The tall, bald one was staring at him, frowning, questions fairly flying from his dark eyes.

Verrain had the urge to cut and run, but with his soaked clothes and his being in plain sight, it would have been foolish. He obviously needed a room for the night and this was the only hotel he had seen.

"Yes, may I help you?"

She was short but full-figured for a Burmese. The *xongyi* was wrapped tightly around her hips and buttocks. The blouse, or *ingyi*, was, as usual, completely transparent, and her dark nipples gleamed behind it.

Verrain knew little Burmese, but he managed with a combination of it, Chinese, and English to get across that he wanted a beer and a room, in that order.

The girl glided away.

"English?" It was the piano player.

"American," Verrain replied.

The man looked up. His smile was thin-lipped over unparted teeth. "American, eh? Interesting. We see few tourists, no Americans, outside this far of Rangoon." His English was chopped up, but good.

Verrain shrugged. "I'm not exactly a tourist. I'm a photographer on an assignment."

"Ah." He tinkled a little more. "You have your visa? Police very bad about visas."

"I have it." Verrain had gone to the consultate right after arriving in Bangkok, and gotten a seven-day visa for Burma just in case. He had three days left on it.

The girl brought the beer. "I fix room."

"Thank you."

She moved over to the five truckers at the table. Verrain tried to watch her, but the piano player was talking again.

"What? . . . I'm sorry."

"She very pretty girl. She my sister Sim Li."

Verrain only nodded and worried his beer. His intentness on the girl could have been construed as interest in the front of her blouse. Actually, he was curious about the rapid-fire conversation between her and the truckers.

"I see your visa and passport, please." The piano player again.

"You?"

"Oh, yes, this my hotel," the little man said with a grin. "I am Sim Dok. This my hotel."

"Oh." Verrain handed them over. The girl moved back by him, flashing him a coy smile with her dark eyes.

Her brother studied Verrain's papers. "Oh, you have enjoyed Burma for four days."

Verrain thought fast. He could have lied, but he would have to get the Rover in the morning.

"No, I just came over tonight, by car. In fact I had to leave it up on the road. A washout."

"I see. Roads very dangerous when monsoon start."

He handed the passport back and returned to his piano-playing.

The five men stood, but only four of them went through the door. The taller, ugly one with the bald pate sauntered toward Verrain. From his height and build, Verrain guessed that there was some European blood mixed in with his Chinese and Burmese ancestry.

"I overhear," he said. "Is shame we missed you on the road. We had truck stuck up there and took another up to pull it out. Had we seen you we would have given you ride."

Verrain smiled. "I saw the truck. Evidently you didn't get it out."

The eyes hooded over. "No. No, we didn't."

Verrain could feel sweat adding to the wetness of his shirt. "Maybe you can give me a hand in the morning when you go back up to get your truck. Some planks across the road . . ."

"Maybe. You didn't notice if any thieves got to our load, did you?"

"Thieves? Load? I think the truck was empty."

The man smiled, but the corners of his lips turned down. Verrain was sure he had not been believed. He would sleep lightly tonight.

The piano player was playing a one-finger melody. The ugly one turned, barked at him in rapid-fire Burmese that Verrain couldn't catch, and stalked out.

There was a light tug on Verrain's elbow. He rolled around on the stool. The girl's smiling face was an inch from his.

"Room is ready. This way, please."

He followed the swaying hips up the stairs and down a dimly lit hall. The room was small and in the rear of the building. She yanked a string hanging from a bare overhead bulb, and Verrain looked it over.

It contained an ancient brass bed with what would be a lumpy mattress, a beat-up dresser with a cracked glass top, a big, overstuffed chair with the stuffing coming out, and some hooks on the wall for a closet.

There were two doors, the one to the hall and another, probably to an adjacent room. Both of them had old-fashioned skeleton-key locks.

"The key?" Verrain asked.

She shrugged. "No key."

He tried the connecting door. It was locked.

"Always locked," she said, and opened the shutters. "You

will need air. It rains but monsoon very hot."

Verrain kicked off his sodden shoes and rubbed his blood-shot eyes. When he dropped his hands and opened his eyes, she was right in front of him, her naturally crimson lips turned in an inviting smile and her brown-tipped breasts molded against the blouse.

"If you wish anything . . . anything at all . . . just call down the stairs."

The inference was there. Verrain wasn't interested. "Sleep, just sleep. Thank you."

She went to the door somewhat reluctantly. Verrain closed it behind her and shoved the overstuffed chair in front of it.

By the time he had stripped off the wet clothes and killed the light, the lack of sleep for over sixty hours had enveloped him.

He went out just like the light, quickly and completely.

The sleep was dreamless. There was no sound, so it must have been the smell. He couldn't place it at first, and then it hit him: perfume.

There was something soft pressed against his back, and hair tickled his cheek. He rolled over, struggling against the pull of sleep, and the perfume got stronger.

"Hello, American. You caressed my body in your sleep. You want to do more awake?"

He sat up. She tugged at his arms, but not very hard.

"Out. I told you I'm not interested."

"Oh? Look at yourself, American. I have already made you interested while you sleep."

Verrain looked down at himself, and jumped from the bed. "Out!"

She kicked the covers from her body and sat up. She was stark naked, all curves and dark hollows. She reached for him, and at the same time shot an anxious glance toward the door.

It was too anxious a glance.

It brought him wide awake. The overstuffed chair had been slid to the side. He tried it. The door was locked. There was a key in the lock of the connecting door on his side. Her clothes were on the chair. Verrain grabbed them.

"Dammit, get dressed and . . ."

The sarong and blouse were mangled, as if they had been ripped from her. A tiny pair of blue panties were shredded in half.

That was when she started screaming.

Verrain dived for his pants. His belt was barely buckled when the hall door shattered inward. At the same time, the girl—still screaming—hurled herself at him, clawing at his face with her nails.

There were three of them, in uniform. One of them grabbed her while the other two got armlocks on Verrain.

She was crying and babbling in Burmese. The policemen looked mean. One of the cops listened intently and turned on Verrain, barking questions.

"I don't speak Burmese," he shouted. "English . . . Chinese . . ."

In fractured Mandarin, the policeman replied, "You will come with us."

"The hell . . ."

The one on his left chopped him, expertly, behind the ear. It didn't put him out, but it made him manageable. The solo one gathered his bags and the rest of his clothes, and the other two half walked, half dragged him down the hall. Doors opened on both sides and heads popped out. One quick look and the doors slammed.

Down the stairs and out the door. He was slammed into

the back seat of a car, with one of them on each side of him. The solo one got in the front.

There was already someone in the driver's seat.

Verrain looked up, forcing his eyes to focus.

It was the ugly Eurasian man with the bald head.

TWO

From the living room of his air-conditioned suite, Nick Carter watched a powerful speedboat pulling a couple of water skiers across the sun-dappled blue of the sea. Faster and faster they went, darting in and out among the white sailboats. Directly below his window, tables with bright umbrellas dotted the seaside terrace and girls in colorful bikinis decorated the hotel's private beach.

He looked up from the sea that rolled between Hong Kong and Kowloon. The cloud-shrouded mountains of mainland China could be seen in the distance. In the forefront, modern hotels, office buildings, and high-rise apartments lined both shores.

Late-afternoon sunshine glinted off the swirling traffic between the buildings and the sea.

Miami Beach, Far East style, Carter thought, and stuck a cigarette between his teeth. He was about to light it, when a new burst of color hit the beach. He grabbed the glasses and brought them to his eyes to make sure.

Bikini, both pieces striped orange and black. Long legs, full figure, heavy black hair up and around her head in coils, an orange flower in her hair behind her ear. A large beach

13

towel that matched the bikini.

Odd colors for the beach, for swimming attire. There couldn't be another like it, especially since it had been made for her.

Carter slipped on a hip-length robe and shoved his feet into a pair of sandals. He buttoned the robe over his scarred upper body as he walked down the hall. In the lobby, he bought a fresh pack of cigarettes at horrible Hong Kong prices, and headed outside and across the boulevard to the beach.

The beaches of Hong Kong would never win any prizes. The sand was coarse and grating, and beyond the hotel area he could see trash being washed ashore. The sea wouldn't dare wash trash ashore on the hotel beach itself, not at $600 a day for a suite.

Carter thanked his lucky stars that it was on AXE's tab.

At ground level, the look was different. The beach was hardly visible for the skin, mostly female. They were everywhere, stacked side by side, heavily oiled, bodies gleaming in the sun.

They were of every color and every size, tall girls, short girls, slim girls, and ample girls. There were girls in small bikinis, teeny bikinis, and no bikinis, at least no tops. Some were blond, some were brunette, but all of them were sexy.

There was hardly a man in sight. But then it was the men who made money in Hong Kong, so the men worked during the day. If they didn't, most of these lovelies wouldn't have a place to go at night.

Carter walked along the water's edge, smoking and looking. Some of the girls looked back directly. Others looked but pretended not to.

And then he spotted her. She had done the best she could to find an open space.

Her eyes were closed to the hot sun. She seemed to be

sleeping. Casually, Carter moved over to her, dropped to a crouch, and admired the view.

She looked even better close up.

A drop of perspiration slid to the end of his nose and fell onto her well-tanned body.

He hadn't planned it, but it was one way of getting her attention. She opened her eyes. They were black, laughing eyes, and her nose wrinkled nicely when she saw him.

"Hello."

"Hi. Pardon my sweat."

"Accidents happen," she said.

"Haven't we met before?"

"How original," she said, smiling, raising a well-manicured hand to shield her eyes.

"Let's see, you're a travel agent here on a familiarization trip." Absently, Carter unbuttoned his beach jacket.

"No, I'm a spy from mainland China here stealing recipes."

"Nick."

"Jillian."

"Nice name. May I occupy the space beside you?"

Casually, with one finger, she pulled aside the jacket. "That's an odd scar. Mind if I touch it?"

"What better way to get acquainted."

The tip of one finger ran the length of the scar from his right nipple down his side to disappear at his trunks.

"You don't have to stop there if you don't want to," he said seriously.

She laughed. "I will, for now. Have a seat."

"Thanks."

He stretched out on the sand beside her and looked around without seeming to. A few of the girls around them were smirking, and an older couple, as white and plump as two beached dolphins, had already lost interest.

Just another good-looking guy trying to pick up a good-looking girl on the beach.

That was how it was supposed to be. But they would keep it up, and eventually she would feed him in natural conversation what he needed to know.

He turned his attention back to her. She was still smiling, now with one eye open.

"Are they so fascinating?" she asked.

"What?"

"My breasts. You're staring at them."

"They're very nice."

"Thank you," she replied. She adjusted the bikini halter and lay back. "Is that a professional judgment?"

"Oh, yes. You see, I'm actually an engineer, design."

"And you design bras?"

"Of course." It was his turn to smile. "Are you on vacation?"

"Part business, part pleasure. Today I have the second shift."

That meant that she would be following and keeping tabs on Rafael Oheda from around six that evening until the wee hours of the morning.

There were three of them assigned to the job. Jillian, whose last name was Sorbonnia, was AXE. She was American, but of Filipino descent. She was stationed in Manila. The other two members of the team were Jane Soong and Leslie Munson. They were both British MI6, and stationed in Hong Kong.

Jillian had picked up Oheda when he flew out of Manila. When they were sure he was headed for Hong Kong, the MI6 people were recruited. It was always easier to operate in someone's backyard if you let him in on it.

Rafael Oheda was a money manager, a fixer, and deal maker. He operated out of Manila, but his fingers reached throughout the Far East. About eighty percent of his dealings were legal, if somewhat unethical. It had been only a few weeks before when U.S. intelligence had learned that the other twenty percent of his work included huge arms purchases for the many rebel groups operating in the Philippine mountains.

A few days earlier, it had come through the grapevine that Oheda was leaving Manila to make a large buy. Since AXE was already on the trail of a big arms purveyor in Southeast Asia, it was thought that the one might uncover the other.

Nick Carter, AXE Killmaster, was given the assignment of tabbing Oheda's contact when the meet was made. The powers that be in D.C.—mainly the crusty head of AXE, David Hawk—had decided that surveillance on Oheda in the first stages should be done by females. Carter had agreed.

"Is your work pleasant?" Carter continued.

"I've been here two days and not a hitch yet."

In forty-eight hours they hadn't lost Oheda once, and the log on him was complete.

"How long will you be in town?"

"From the looks of things, it could be at least a few more days."

Oheda didn't seem to be in much of a hurry to meet the seller.

"Carter was about to speak again, when a buzzer in her beach bag went off.

"Excuse me, I have to make a call. Oh, would you watch my things?"

"Sure."

She made a nice picture of fluid movement going across the sand toward the phone booth. Idly, Carter glanced around the beach to see if anyone was more than normally interested in her.

Other than appreciative glances, that was it.

Five minutes later she was back, shaking the sand out of her towel and stowing it in the bag.

"That was my associate in the hotel. She's heard from my other partner . . ."

Carter nodded his understanding.

"It seems that all three of us will be needed in Macao this evening."

"Too bad," Carter said. "Then your business may be coming to a close?"

She nodded. "It looks that way." She started to move away.

"Maybe we'll run into each other again."

Over her shoulder, with a smile that was more than just business, "Let's hope so."

Carter waited until she hit the street, then he took off toward his own hotel.

He checked his watch.

With a shower and quick shave he should still make the next boat to Macao.

He was sure Jillian Sorbonnia was thinking the same thing.

Macao is a hotbed. The colony is basically independent, but it still retains its ties to mother Portugal. At heart it is Chinese with a flavor all its own.

It has always been—and always will be—a hotbed of intrigue. The Chinese spy on the British. The Russians spy on the Chinese. And the Americans and British spy on everyone.

There was a fity-fifty chance that Carter would be recognized, but he had to take it.

The hydrofoil moved at a fast clip along the Pearl River estuary skirting mainland China. The night was dark and humid. The view through the open roof of the lounge was one of black sky and brilliant stars. Now and then they would pass crawling fishing or trading junks or an occasional Chinese gunboat.

In a corner, several tables from the bar where Carter sat, Jillian Sorbonnia sipped a drink. Only once since they had left Hong Kong had the woman glanced his way. Their eyes had met for an instant and that was it.

Carter had also spotted Leslie Munson. He had never met any of the three women in person before the afternoon's encounter with Jillian, but he had studied their photographs.

At forty, Munson had fifteen years on Jillian and the third woman, Jane Soong. But she still had much of the aristocratic beauty of her youth. It was combined with the grace and sophistication of a woman at ease at the highest social levels in Hong Kong. She was active in society, and instantly recognizable. She moved back and forth between the two totally divergent cities of London and Hong Kong as though one was simply a suburb of the other. She had been with MI6 since her mid-twenties.

For the evening's pursuit she had commandeered a young escort who looked as if he had just stepped out of the embassy's personnel file. From the conversation Carter could hear over the tiny receiver in his ear, he was boring Leslie Munson to death.

They were outside the lounge at the rail of the main forward deck. Beyond them, Carter could see the lighthouse in the old fort of Guia. Then they were rounding the breakwater and coming into the pier.

"Nick, you be the first one off." It was Jillian's voice breaking in on the chatter of Munson's escort.

Carter dropped some Hong Kong dollars on the bar and headed for the lower decks. By the time he got there, the hydrofoil was tied up and they were swinging the gangway over. A line of disembarking passengers had already formed.

Carter joined it and moved ashore.

Briskly, he walked toward the huge jai alai stadium across the street. Turning up the volume on his receiver, he lit a cigarette and waited.

Jillian was the first off. Carter saw her move to the side, alone, and raise a tissue to her lips.

"Jane, can you talk?"

"I am in the casino of the Lisboa Hotel. This is the third casino he has hit tonight and he seems to be looking for someone."

"Check," Jillian replied. "I hope everyone got that."

Carter moved off as Jillian got in the taxi line. In his ear he heard Leslie Munson's escort: "Shall we try our luck at the Hyatt?"

"Oh, no, darling," Leslie replied. "I much prefer the Lisboa . . . so much more 'old world'!"

Carter smiled. Everyone was heading for the Lisboa.

Two blocks farther on, he hailed a pedicab. Because of the slower mode of transportation, he would arrive at the huge hotel-casino complex a good ten minutes after the two women.

And that was as it should be.

Rafael Oheda hunched over the table listlessly. He rarely gambled, so the winning or losing cards dealt him were pretty much all the same.

His fat, ruddy face gleamed with perspiration under the harsh lights. It was a lined and drooping face, with thick black eyebrows that pressed down on the squinting black eyes as if by their own weight. His nose was fleshy and he had heavy lips that stretched insensitively around a dead cigar. The total effect was ugliness and a kind of lazy cunning.

He had been at this silly game in three different casinos

for as many hours, and he was getting angry. He had cooled his heels in the Hong Kong hotel for longer than he had desired. Then the phone call had come at last to distress him even more.

"Take the four o'clock ferry to Macao. Gamble," the voice had said.

"Gamble . . . where?"

"Where one usually gambles—in the casinos."

"How will I know you?"

"You won't. I will find you."

Ridiculous, Oheda thought, raking in his winnings and betting again. Secrecy was one thing. That he could understand. But this, this constant fog, was something else. No names, nothing on paper, nothing in the form of an agreement or deal made over a telephone, money in specified blind accounts, nothing that would leave a paper trail.

Oheda was a businessman, and as such used to knowing with whom he was doing business.

But not these people. They told you nothing.

But they did have the exact goods that Oheda's clients wanted. "Deal with them," he had been told. "Earn your commission for once."

So he was in Macao and he would deal with this voiceless, faceless, nameless man. After all, his commission would be nearly a quarter of a million dollars.

He won again.

"Senhor is lucky tonight."

Oheda glanced to his left. He hadn't noticed the woman sliding onto the stool beside him. She was striking, and could have been attractive were she a little less severe. Her dark brown hair was drawn back tightly from her forehead, a braided coronet across her head. Her almond-shaped eyes were dark, rather small, and they looked straight into him.

"Sorry, I don't speak Portuguese."

"I just commented that you are very lucky. Would you mind if I side bet your square, as well as my own?"

Oheda shrugged and dismissed her. He had no interest in women. Money was his mistress, and the accumulation of it provided his orgasms.

For the next three hands she played her own square as well as Oheda's. They both lost.

Oheda put a lighter to his cigar.

"Would you mind?"

He lit her cigarette. For the briefest of seconds her hand held his, steadying the flame. He felt the folded slip of paper slip into his palm and closed his fingers over it.

Two hands later the woman excused herself from the table. She tipped the dealer and left.

Oheda waited a few moments and headed for the men's room.

"Jane, Leslie . . . he's out of the men's room and moving," Jillian said, moving herself toward the front entrance to the casino.

"I've got him," Jane Soong replied, "the side exit."

Leslie Munson's voice was slightly garbled. "Excuse me, darling . . . the drinks, you know."

At a table two spaces down from the one where Oheda had been playing, Carter watched the women slip from the casino. He knew they would have cars stationed outside to follow Oheda. He would wait, checking to make sure they weren't being followed in turn.

Five minutes later he heard Jillian's voice again, and knew that Oheda had taken a cab. He pocketed his chips and hit the front door.

He was just in time to see the woman who had been sitting beside Oheda slip into the rear of a black Mercedes.

Two rough-looking Chinese types were in the front.

It didn't take a genius to figure out that the woman had made contact with Oheda.

In the distance, Carter could see the three women closing in behind the taxi carrying Oheda. They would fall in and fall out behind him, taking turns so they wouldn't be spotted.

The maneuver would be spotted in no time by the three in the Mercedes.

Carter wasted no time. He unbuttoned his top button, loosened his tie, and staggered forward just as the Mercedes pulled from the curb.

Just as it was picking up speed, Carter stepped from between two cars. His hips glanced off the side of the front fender and, just at the same time, he slapped the fender hard with his right palm.

The effect was perfect . . . lots of sound, a howl of brakes and pain, and Carter's body rolling in front of the car.

Within seconds a crowd had gathered, and through slitted eyes Carter could see two uniformed police pushing their way through the ring of people.

THREE

Oheda followed the directions on the note to the letter even as it galled him. He changed cabs three times, and had the last one let him out at the plaza in front of the Cathedral of St. Paul.

He waited until the cab drove away, and then crossed the wide boulevard. On such a soft, warm night, there were a lot of strollers, and the tables outside the cafés were crowded.

A few steps into a side street entirely made up of cafés, he spotted the Tivoli. The table he was looking for was the third from the right on the outer edge.

There was a man sitting quietly at the table, alone. He was sipping a Campari and soda with the expression of someone who had learned to savor the small pleasures of life when they came his way. He had smooth, light brown hair and the ruddy face of a man who burned in the sun without ever getting a tan. With his narrow pointed nose and very wide jawbones, there was something jolly about his face. But the look ended in his dull green eyes. Cold and alert, they sized Oheda up as he approached.

Oheda was surprised. He had expected to meet an Oriental, not a Caucasian. He took a chair.

"I am Oheda."

"I know who ya are, mate."

The thick cockney accent also surprised Oheda. The man took out a torn half of a ten-pound note and smoothed it on the table. His hands were those of a workman, broad and flat with thick fingers. They looked like clumsy hands, but the look in the green eyes said differently.

"You wouldn't have half a tenner, would ya, mate?"

Oheda took his half from an inside pocket. He put it down, and the other man fitted the two halves together. They fit perfectly.

"Where'd ya get it, mate?"

"Look here, is all this necessary? I don't have time—"

"Then you'll have to make the time, mate. We do things a certain way, we do."

Oheda sighed. "Manila. It was slipped under the door of my apartment in a white envelope."

"Good, mate."

"Surely you're not . . ."

"Naw, I ain't the man. I just take ya to him. I'm kind of a watchdog."

"Do watchdogs have names?"

Amusement crept into the green eyes. "Sure. Carl. You look a little nervous, Mr. Oheda."

"I'm not used to doing business this way."

Carl chuckled. "That's probably because you don't do as much of this kind of business as we do. Ya got a gun?"

"Of course not," Oheda sputtered.

"I do," Carl replied. "Let's go."

Oheda followed him deeper into the ill-lit street. The man was extremely light on his feet for a man of his solid bulk.

They went through a cobbled alley and turned into another short, dimly lit street. Cars were triple-parked on both sides, which was the only way of solving an unsolvable parking problem.

Suddenly a short Chinese girl in a skintight, bright red *cheongsam*, the sides of the high-necked dress slit to the tops of her thighs, stepped out of a doorway. She moved directly to Carl and slipped her thighs over one of his and her arms about his neck.

"Chi Chi, good time. You want?"

"Get away, you whore," Carl growled, disentwining himself.

The girl's hands slid down his body. "I do your friend, two for one . . . what you say?"

"Get your bloody hands off me!" Carl got the flat of his hand against her chest and shoved her aside.

"Bloody English shit," the girl hissed, and walked quickly away.

Carl unlocked the doors of a dark blue Honda sedan and slid behind the wheel. Oheda got in the passenger seat. The door was scarcely shut behind him when the car lurched forward.

At the corner, they saw the Chinese hooker in the red dress. As they passed, she raised her middle finger in the international salute and stuck out her tongue.

"Jillian, can you hear me?" Jane Soong asked.

"Loud and clear."

"I put the beeper on the short stocky one."

"We've got him and it's coming in clear. They're heading toward the inner harbor. Walk toward the Avenida Almeida Ribiero and we'll pick you up."

The young woman in the tight red dress took off at a fast pace, whistling to herself.

• • •

In the ambulance, Carter could barely hear their voices. The distance was too great to make out words. When they faded even more, he suddenly snapped the belt around his chest and sat up.

Up to that moment, the female paramedic had been almost dozing beside the gurney. Now she came alive and grabbed Carter's shoulders.

"No, no, you must lie down!"

"I'm fine," Carter said, unbuckling the strap from his legs. "Tell the driver to stop."

"No, you must—"

Carter grabbed both her wrists, squeezing just enough to be painful. "Tell him."

She squealed in pain and barked at the driver. He turned in his seat, bewildered, but he pulled the ambulance to the curb.

The ambulance had barely stopped when Carter jammed a wad of bills into the woman's hand. "That should take care of both of you and the costs."

He was out the back door and running before the driver was out of his seat.

The dodge would hold up the three in the Mercedes, but there was no guarantee that they didn't have a backup.

In the open, Jillian's voice was coming in a little better. He couldn't catch everything, but he heard enough to bring a smile to his face.

One of them had been able to plant a bug. Now Oheda could be trailed from a distance. It wouldn't make any difference if there was a backup to the Mercedes.

Two more turns brought him to a cabstand.

"São Tiago," Carter growled.

"Sim."

The flag dropped and away they went.

•   •   •

Carl cut in and out of traffic with a skillful disregard for the rules of the road. Every few seconds he would glance into the rearview mirror.

He tooled the car around the huge square of Governor's House, and headed back toward the inner city. Again he checked the rearview.

"Is someone following us?" Oheda asked.

"Not yet," Carl replied, and then grinned evilly across the car. "And you'd better hope no one does, mate."

Oheda's face flushed.

"We're back on the Almeida Ribiero," Jillian said, watching the green dot moving along on the tiny screen in front of her. "And we're heading right back to the Hotel Lisboa."

"Do you think they're on to us?" Leslie Munson asked from the driver's seat.

"Not likely," Jane Soong said from the car trailing them.

"What now?" Leslie asked.

"Damn, they're taking the bridge over to Taipa," Jillian said.

"They'll spot us," Leslie replied. "If they see two cars coming off the bridge this time of night, they'll surely check."

The island of Taipa was small but well populated with the University of East Asia campus, two high-rise hotels, and vast, expensive estates. Its only connection with the mainland peninsula of Macao was a mile-long dead-end bridge.

Jillian was trying to make a split-second decision, when it was made for her. The tiny green dot was about in the middle of the bridge and it had slowed to a crawl. They were either checking their rear or waiting for a backup.

"Pull in here—now!" she said. "Nick, if you can hear me, we're in the front parking lot of the Hotel Lisboa."

The second car pulled up beside them and Jane Soong rolled down her window. "What now?"

"We wait," Jillian replied. "Unless something has happened to Carter, he should be close behind us."

"And if something has happened to him?"

"We still wait," Jillian said firmly. "Once Oheda is tracked, it's Carter's show. Those are our orders."

Good girl, Carter thought with a smile. "Driver?"

"Sim?"

"Isn't there a high road just this side of the Taipa bridge entrance?"

"Sim, senior."

"Go there."

"But I thought—"

"I changed my mind."

They were at the circle of the A-Ma Temple. With a shrug, the driver spun the wheel and they headed across the peninsula.

A mile off the main road, a graveled drive curved up the slope of a dark, wooded hill. Halfway up, the way was blocked by a high gate made of thick iron bars, set in a thick stone wall.

"I suppose you're going to blindfold me as well," Oheda said caustically.

Carl leered. "No need. Once we get your money and you get your goods, you can tell the whole world what we look like and it won't do any good."

A chain dangled just inside the iron bars of the gate. Carl reached in and yanked on it. Somewhere in the darkness within the walls, there was the bonging of what sounded like a church bell.

Instantly, floodlights went on outside the gates, catching

them and the car in their glare. But on the other side of the
gate it stayed pitch black. Inside that blackness dogs began
howling. They weren't the kind of dogs you'd want to meet
without a gun.

There was a small speaker set in the wall beside the gate.
Carl spoke into it. About a minute went by, and the dogs
stopped howling. But the area inside the gate stayed dark.
After another minute two shadowy figures appeared on the
other side of the gate. Stocky men with peasant clothes and
faces. One of them held a sawed-off shotgun. The other
had a long-barreled revolver in one hand; his other hand
was controlling two dogs on chain leashes.

They studied Carl and Oheda through the bars. Then the
one with the dogs moved aside, out of sight. The other
unlocked the gate and got all his weight behind pulling at
one of the bars. The gate swung open heavily on well-oiled
hinges.

As they got back in the car, Oheda asked Carl, "How
many troops have you got in here?"

"Not exactly troops, mate," Carl said as he drove through
the gate, following a path that curved upward. "More like
survival specialists. Ever hear of the Toong Lu?"

"No."

"In the old days, they were a society in Burma formed
by emigrating Chinese. They were all trained to a fine edge
to protect the rich old Chinese from the British when old
King Thibaw handed the country over to the Brits."

"What were they trained to do?"

"Obey and kill," Carl replied. "Believe me, mate, these
boys would make your bloody jungle guerrillas in the Philippines look like a bunch of old ladies."

He pulled into a level area hedged on two sides by tall
palms. He parked between a Jeep and two cars, a Rover
limousine and a Fiat sedan. What looked like a miniature

castle squatted on top of the hill above: a big pile of old stone, with turrets jutting toward the night sky, and no lights showing from within. Shutters were closed across all the windows.

Oheda followed Carl up the path to the front door. The door was heavy wood with big iron studs. Carl banged it with a bronze knocker in the shape of a tiger's head. The lock clicked, and Carl pushed the door open. They entered a small foyer with walls and floor of pale gray marble. No one else was there.

Carl led the way through a dim corridor into a big, high-ceilinged room with priceless Persian carpets covering most of the parquet floor. There seemed to be a lot of big, heavy chairs, sofas, and tables that didn't go with the two suits of armor flanking the wide doorway. A huge stone fireplace took up most of one wall. The other walls were darkly paneled, covered with oil paintings, antiqued mirrors in ornate gold frames, crossed swords, engraved shields.

Looking somehow entirely at ease in this museum, a man wearing a gold silk dressing gown and black felt slippers put aside a half-smoked cigar, rose from the depths of an overstuffed wing chair, and extended a slim hand to Oheda.

All of him was slim. But his handshake was firm. And the light brown eyes that looked into Oheda's dark ones were dead level. They made the Filipino shudder.

"Good evening, Mr. Oheda. I am so sorry for all this inconvenience, but I assure you it is necessary. A drink?"

"Whiskey, please."

"Carl, a whiskey for our guest. Please, Mr. Oheda, sit."

Oheda followed him to a deep sofa in front of the fireplace, studying him discreetly. The man was entirely bald. It added strength and age to his deeply tanned but unlined face.

And then it hit Oheda. There were no scalp lines, no facial lines, and the eye sockets were too deep to be natural.

The man noticed Oheda's frown, and chuckled. "A mask, Mr. Oheda, such as the special effects people use in the cinema. Clever, eh?"

"Yes, yes, very, Mr. . . . ?"

"No need for names, Mr. Oheda. I'm sure you would not have contacted my organization had you not thoroughly checked out our reliability first."

Oheda was uncomfortable and he couldn't hide it. He took the drink from Carl and downed half of it with one swallow.

"Well," he said, gripping the glass, "I have a list of my client's needs—"

"Please, please, Mr. Oheda. Plenty of time for business later, after we have dined. There is an excellent dinner awaiting us in the dining room."

"I'm not hungry," Oheda rasped.

The man in the strange rubbery mask smiled. "Yes, you are. Shall we go?"

The man was taller than Oheda, but lighter by fifty pounds. Yet his grip on the Filipino's arm was like two steel pincers. Oheda was sure that if the man wanted to, he could snap his arm like a twig.

"How long do we sit here, Senhor? My shift was up twenty minutes ago."

"A little longer," Carter said, adding to the pile of Hong Kong dollars on the front seat by the driver.

And then he saw it: the Mercedes sedan. It had been parked in the cutoff on the other side of the bridge. He couldn't see into the rear seat, but he could see the two men in the front.

"Now we can go."

"Where?"

"The front parking lot of the Hotel Lisboa."

The driver sighed with relief and the car rolled down the hill. Three turns and ten minutes later, Carter stepped from the taxi and waited until it drove off toward the center city.

He had already spotted them on the other side of the parking lot, away from the lights.

"Jillian," he said with a smile, crawling into the rear seat, "you're even lovelier in clothes. And you're Jane Soong. How do you do? Carter. Nick Carter."

Her pretty face wrinkled into a smile. "A pleasure to meet you. I have heard of your work."

"Leslie Munson."

"How do you do?" Carter said. "What happened to your escort?"

Leslie shrugged. "He'll go back to Hong Kong with a broken heart. He's used to it."

Jillian was tapping the screen in front of her. "Suppose we can get down to it?"

"Of course," Carter quipped. "One of you was tagged."

The three of them exchanged guilty glances. "Which one?" Jillian asked.

"Don't know," he replied, "but my guess is, it was you. You turned right out of the hotel. That's the way they were going when I stopped them."

"You made contact?" Leslie asked.

"You might say that," Carter replied with a low chuckle, and turned back to Jillian. "You got them pinpointed?"

She nodded. "On the far side of Taipa, beyond the university. It's all big estates over there, probably a lot of security."

Carter started taking off his dark trousers and dinner jacket. Beneath them he wore a tight suit. "Who did Oheda meet?"

Jane Soong replied with a description of the short, stocky man. "I got his picture."

"Good. Did you happen to get a picture of the Oriental woman who got a light from him at the last casino?"

"I got a picture of everyone he even looked at," Jane replied.

"Very good. Did you bring my tools?"

From the front seat, Leslie Munson handed him a stiletto in a chamois sheath, and a 9mm Luger in a shoulder rig. Attached to the rig was a silencer and an oilskin watertight wrap for the Luger. Also attached to the rig, fitted on the opposite side of the holster, was a slim night camera.

"How does it go from here?" Jillian asked.

"You," Carter said, "stay on this side of the bridge. We'll stay in contact so you can raise some hell for us if anything goes wrong. Jane, you and Leslie will go with me."

"If we don't know for sure that it was Jillian who was spotted, how will we know which car to take?"

"We're not taking a car," Carter replied. "Head toward the marina. I'm going to steal a boat."

FOUR

"That's it!" Leslie Munson said, pointing toward a distant set of lights barely discernible in the gloom.

"You're sure?" Carter asked.

"Positive. It's the one on the hills, with the lights."

"Okay," he said, attaching the tiny mike and battery pack inside his wet suit and making sure the earplug receiver was in place. "You two keep circling out here, small arcs. Don't get any closer into shore."

"Are you swimming in?" Jane asked.

"That's the general idea," Carter replied. "They see that sail within a half mile of their pier, and my guess is they'll investigate. Going in on the ocean side is always the safest way, but not worth a damn without surprise."

Without another word, he rolled over the side and struck out. He took it a hundred yards at a time before resting and then changing his stroke.

A quarter mile out, he bobbed with only his eyes above the surface. It was a large estate: the ocean side had a good thousand feet of frontage with high stone walls on each side leading down to the water.

There was another wall on the far side with two walk-through gates. The good thing was the beach on the ocean side of the wall. It was narrow, only about twenty feet. If he could wait until a cloud covered the moon, he could probably get across it and over the wall without being spotted.

Of course, to get to the beach he would have to get by the big oceangoing yacht tied to a pier jutting out into the ocean.

Whoever this boy is, Carter thought, *he's a security freak.*

He struck out again, this time with a breast stroke to keep down any ripples in the water. The glow of a cigarette told him that someone was walking the deck of the yacht, back and forth.

Without even seeing the man's face, Carter made odds that it was turned constantly out to sea.

He went under and moved with long butterfly strokes until his hands touched solid. He surfaced carefully and saw the long, needle-nosed bow arching over him. He worked his way back on the starboard side. Above him, the hull gently rocked against the rubber bumpers attached to the pier.

When the brass-railed gangway was directly above him, he waited. Suddenly the guard appeared; there had been no sound from the guard's deck shoes.

Carter made no movement as the cigarette arched outward from the man's fingers. It hissed out less than six inches from the Killmaster's face.

He checked the area between the rear wall and the villa. He could see movement now and then in the trees, but they wouldn't see him if he went over the side just forward of the superstructure amidships.

He waited until he was sure the guard was at the bow, and then he worked his way up the struts of the pier. It would be tricky. The sea was calm, but the yacht was riding the natural swells of the tide. All he had to do was misjudge his timing going up, and he would be crushed between the hull and the pier.

"Chung-sa, wayli ung lai oww?"

The voice had come from somewhere belowdecks, maybe the galley. So, Carter thought, there were two of them. The roving guard answered in a language that sounded like bastard Chinese. Carter couldn't begin to understand it.

There was a soft, rustling sound and the boat yawed away from the pier. Carter grabbed the taut mooring line and worked his way up and over. Just as he hit the deck on his belly and pulled his legs after him, the sound repeated and the bow mashed against the bumpers where his legs had been a millisecond before.

Wiping the sweat from his face, he moved into a groove of the superstructure and pulled a lightweight rubber face mask from under his top. It was like a skintight ski mask with holes for eyes and mouth.

The two men again shouted to each other. Carter still couldn't understand, but he thought he caught the word "tea" from down below. From the outside guard's tone, Carter surmised a negative reply.

He moved forward in a crouch, coming up directly behind the man who was trying to light another cigarette. Carter caught him full in the throat with the knuckles of his left hand, and nailed him with the calloused side of his right on the way down.

He caught the body and then eased it gently to the deck. He checked. There was no pulse. Carter cursed under his breath. He would try to keep the other one below alive long enough for a few questions.

This one was loaded: a flare gun, a U.S. Army-issue .45 automatic, an M-16 altered for silencer, and an ugly Tong knife with a blade coming out both ends.

Not your usual hardware for a plain old-fashioned body-

guard, Carter mused as he snapped a shot of the dead man's face with the night camera and moved forward, being careful to keep the superstructure between himself and the beach.

"*"Chung, fou un loi?"*

Again Carter didn't understand, but it made no difference. He dropped through the hatch into the galley without touching the handrail or the ladder. In both hands in front of him he held the Luger.

The man was short but powerfully built, with a teacup in one hand and a soup ladle in the other. He wore only a pair of long Chinese shorts, and his body was completely hairless.

"Speak above a whisper and I will make your mother mourn and your woman a widow," Carter growled.

Obviously the man understood Mandarin. Slowly his arms went outward and lifted. He seemed to fold, but Carter could see the tension in his body and knew it was an act.

"If you are a thief," the man said, "you are a fool."

"I'll be the judge of that. So many guards for one house, your master must keep a fortune here."

"You are a fool."

"Your friend, above?" Carter said.

"Chung?"

Carter nodded. "He sleeps with his fathers. How many in the villa?"

Instead of answering, the man attacked, faster than a cobra, faster than anything Carter had ever seen.

He sprang like a whippet from a flat-footed position, his two hands at Carter's ankles and his shoulder crashing against the Killmaster's knees.

Carter went to his back before he knew he'd been hit, his spine painfully striking the ladderwell. He felt the air shoot from his lungs as his finger instinctively squeezed the Luger's trigger.

The gun fired once with a *poof* sound. He could have sworn the muzzle was against the man's head, but the slug struck the opposite bulkhead and the Luger clattered to the deck behind him.

The stiletto was Carter's next thought, but the man was unbelievably fast. Before Carter could activate the spring in the chamois sheath, the man had wrenched the rig around so that the blade clattered harmlessly to the deck.

Now the man's hands were working up his body, pounding Carter's stomach, tearing savagely at his face, trying to get through to his throat.

This one, Carter thought, *is an expert. He knows where to go to exert the quickest and harshest punishment, and when the time comes, he'll know how to get the kill!*

Carter jerked his hips upward, unseating the man astride him and twisting onto his stomach. The hands returned to his throat from behind. Lowering his head, he brought his knees under him, straight-armed the deck, and rose to his feet. The man was still behind him with his left arm hooked around his neck, his right fist pounding his kidneys.

He dropped to his knees again, jerking him forward and down, and reached up for his head. He found it and took hold. He came over Carter's shoulder, somersaulting in the air, and struck the deck with the full length of his body. But he was quick. Before Carter could pin him, he was away and turning at the wall.

This is no good, Carter thought. *The guy knows every trick in the book and he's fast, too fast!* It was as if the art of killing was just that, an art, the only thing he knew.

And a second thought struck the Killmaster. The man hadn't even tried to raise an alarm. That's how sure he was of his skills.

Carter started groping for the Luger or the stiletto, but he could neither see nor feel either one.

A blow to the side of his face turned him around and sent him staggering. The other man was after him before he recovered his balance. A heel in the small of his back slammed him against the wall and brought him to his knees with the feeling that his body had been broken in two.

The second kick caught him a glancing blow on the nape of the neck. His head crackled and went numb, though he could still feel the raw half of his face that the rough bulkhead had abraded.

He twisted on his knees in time to receive the third kick in the stomach.

The leering guard closed in on him then, striking rapidly at his face with both hands. They hurt, but they didn't rock him hard. That was wonderful. The man was fast and tricky, but he couldn't hit. All Carter had to do was take the punishment and concentrate on getting to his feet.

The trouble was that his legs were hard to handle. And he couldn't concentrate on them properly with the heels of those deadly hands constantly seeking a death blow to his throat.

Carter flung himself up and out, trying to butt the smaller man's face with his head. Again the man's reaction and speed was awesome. He stepped just far enough and cuffed Carter to the deck with a rabbit punch.

Before the deadly feet could connect with his spine, the Killmaster managed to roll away and raise the weight of his body with his legs. The man caught him on the point of the chin with the heel of his hand almost before Carter's hands left the deck.

Carter staggered away from a second blow, and managed to get a solid kick that connected with a thigh but missed the groin. The guard spun but immediately recovered.

"You're good," Carter growled, feeling the heat of the stove near his back.

The other man grinned, showing yellow teeth. "I am Toong Lu," he hissed, and came in for the kill.

"Good for you," Carter said, spinning and grabbing the pot of boiling soup from the stove.

He emptied all but an inch or two of the pot's contents across the man's face and chest. Then, before the man could cry out in rage and pain, Carter caught him between the eyes with all his force. The guard hit the bulkhead and slid down inch by inch. But before he was on the deck, the Killmaster delivered the last punch, a straight-arm to the throat with bent knuckles.

The windpipe collapsed and he fell to the deck, his face sideways, the eyes fixed.

Carter dropped to his knees himself, gulping in air.

Close, he thought, very close. No more trying to get information when he got ashore. From now on he would shoot first. Whatever Toong Lu was, it was bad medicine.

He gathered the Luger and the stiletto and went topside. Carefully, he moved aft on his belly and slid into the water. Swimming slowly, with only his eyes above the water, he went in and waited.

It was a full fifteen minutes before another cloud passed in front of the moon. Just as he was tensing his body for the run, he saw the two guards on the other side of the stone wall. One was walking around the swimming pool, the other was moving away from him along the right wall.

Accompanying both guards on taut leashes were big, black Dobermans.

Cute, Carter thought, *real cute.*

He backpedaled and went under. Back at the yacht, he went topside just as he had before, and darted down into the galley. The stove was gas, fed by two tanks on deck with the feed lines running through the bulkhead.

He closed all the portholes and hatches, then, across the

galley from the stove, he started a small fire. When it was going good, he cranked on the oven and all four burners to full. In the enclosed space, he figured it would take about five minutes for the gas to blow.

This time, back in the water, he swam to the far corner of the property. When he was flat against the wall, he flipped on the mike.

"Leslie?"

"Yes, we're here."

"In a minute or two, there's going to be a big blow. I'm going in under cover of it. Both of you sail around to the other side of the island and come in. You pick me up there. Use the diesel. The hell with noise now."

"But how are you getting around the island?"

"By limousine, I hope . . ."

The explosion wasn't huge, but the fire was. Orange flame leaped skyward from the blown portholes and ate its way through the first deck.

Just as Carter hoped, guards and dogs ran through the gate and down the pier. In the confusion, he went over the wall. He dropped to the ground in a crouched run, and moved through the trees toward the house.

Four armed men and a woman—the same woman Carter had seen with Oheda at the casino and in the Mercedes—came through the rear door.

Carter adjusted the camera and got a shot of each of them as they ran toward the rear wall. When they were past him, he moved closer to the house, staying in the dense shrubbery for cover.

"C'mon, c'mon!" Carter hissed aloud.

He knew he would have only a few minutes, probably not more than three, to get a photo of Oheda's host. By then, one of the guards would spot the bodies and put everything together.

And then, as if it were a prayer answered, Oheda and a tall man emerged from the house and stood by the pool.

Carter snapped away.

Out of the corner of his eye, he could see the guards running back from the yacht. Both of them were shouting, but Carter couldn't understand the words.

But the tall one in the dressing gown did. He turned, shouted angrily at Oheda, and darted back into the house.

Carter had what he came for. It was time to go. He ran to the darkness of the side wall and followed it to the front of the villa. At the circular drive, he cut across toward the parked vehicles.

There was one guard. He stood by the Rover, the M-16 in his hands raking the front lawn. Carter was on him before he could turn.

The Killmaster fired point-blank.

The two slugs took him out. Carter grabbed the M-16 and ran around the Rover to look.

The keys were in the ignition.

Lights were coming on all over the place now, and he could hear shouting from the adjacent estates.

He scrambled into the car and reached for the ignition. Just as the engine fired, the front door of the villa burst open and two men came through.

The tires spun and squealed as the big car shot forward and Carter snapped on the headlights. The twin beams sliced through the darkness ahead, illuminating the closed gate.

He floored the Rover and headed straight for it. Twenty feet from the gate he made a ball of himself in the seat and steered by memory.

He hit. The gate held for an instant, the car's engine howling and its back tires screaming. Then the gate gave and he was through.

Upright, he used the butt of the Luger to smash a peephole in the shattered windshield.

Two local residents were walking along the road, talking and craning their necks to see the fire. They stopped, looking at the Rover in surprise, then in growing fright, as it closed in on them.

When they realized that the big car was not about to stop or swerve, they both took headers into the bushes.

Carter took his foot off the accelerator and pumped the brake for a right turn. He hoped that the road coming up would take him across the island.

He glanced to the left, then whipped the car right and floored it again. The rear tires spun and the ass end fishtailed from side to side as it gathered momentum.

The speedometer needle crept to the right and hovered over eighty. The bright spots of lights at the entrances to drives flickered past on both sides. The car flashed through an intersection, lifting and becoming almost airborne across the crown of a cross street, then settled back to the pavement.

There was a long, slow curve to the left, and the tires squealed as the right side of the car settled. The street straightened out again, and the Rover roared toward another intersection.

Another car started through the intersection, braked abruptly, and skidded sideways. Carter swerved and missed the car by inches. He got a glimpse of open mouths and white faces in the windows. The car became light on its wheels again on the crown in the intersection, and it tried to skid as it settled. Carter pressed on the accelerator to put traction on the rear wheels, got the car back under control, then eased up on the accelerator and brought the speedometer needle back down to eighty.

A car came out of a driveway ahead and braked to a

sliding stop in the street, and Carter swerved to avoid it. The car skidded across the two wide, brightly lighted lanes and brushed the curb at the side of the center divider. The rear end began trying to drift around. Carter brought the car back under control, accelerating and shifting through the gears. The avenue curved to the left, then straightened out again.

The Rover's headlights had been smashed by the gate. In the rearview mirror, Carter spotted two headlights dancing behind him. From the configuration, it looked like the Jeep.

So, he thought, they were coming after him. His first guess was that they would let him run and clear out themselves.

The rearview mirror trembled from the vibration of the car, and the headlights behind were a blur of light in it. Carter sat back in the seat and held the steering wheel at arm's length, the accelerator pressed to the floor. The sound of the powerful engine rose to a throbbing drone, the speedometer needle sinking to the right.

The guardrails became a dark, mottled blur, their glinting cat's eyes melting together into a gleaming streak as wind screamed around the bent right-front fender and the rumpled hood fluttered. The speedometer swung past one hundred as Carter eased up slightly on the accelerator and held it steady.

And then he saw it, the ocean, about two hundred yards ahead. Off to the right was a huge parking lot for the swimming beach it fronted, and about fifty yards out in the water, idling along, was the boat.

He flipped on the mike. "Leslie, can you hear me?"

"Yes."

"I've got company. I'll be a minute or two. Keep your present speed and course."

"Will do."

Carter veered right without slackening speed, sailed over the embankment, and came down like a sodden tank in the parking lot. The springs bottomed out and the tires howled as the rear end drifted around to the left in a controlled skid.

The big car was still rocking when Carter grabbed the M-16 and rolled out the door.

The Jeep was still coming fast and furious. The driver was going to pull Carter's stunt right up and over the embankment.

The Killmaster pulled the rifle on full auto and brought it to his shoulder.

He waited until the Jeep was in the air, and then fired. The windshield shredded and the driver's head lurched backward, his hands leaving the wheel.

The Jeep came down at a crazy angle, the front wheels doing a crazy wobbling action.

The tires squealed, and then there was a metallic screech as the front tires exploded and the rims hit the asphalt. It nosed over and slammed down onto its roof with a crash of crumpling metal and shattering glass.

The sound was still in the air as Carter dropped the M-16 and ran for the water. He hit the surf in a flat-out dive and swam with long groping strokes.

Jane Soong was at the tiller. When she spotted him, she heeled over and cut ten yards off his distance.

Without cutting speed, Carter caught the bow, heaved himself up, and fell onto the deck at Leslie Munson's feet.

"I'll say this for you, you put on one hell of a show," she chuckled.

"Don't I, though?" Carter gasped, grinning. "Pour the coals to this tub, no running lights. Let's get the hell out of here!"

FIVE

"Shit," Carter growled, and heaved the enlarged photograph back across the desk.

"My sentiments exactly," Jillian Sorbonnia said, rising and moving to the bar for her third drink since the session started.

Richard Garfield, AXE station chief, gave up trying to rub away the weariness in his eyes and leaned back in his chair. "You did the best you could, Nick. You got the pictures. That's what you went in for."

Carter looked down at the blowup again, and grimaced. The tall, distinguished man in the dressing gown stared back at him from behind what was obviously a rubber theatrical mask.

"Any ID on the others?" he asked.

"None. We're still trying on the woman. She's probably the best bet, but that could take weeks."

"What about the villa?" Jillian asked from the bar.

"Nothing. It's owned by a wealthy sheep rancher in Australia. He hardly ever uses it, rents it out when the price is right. This particular rental was to Hempstead Mining Limited, South Africa."

49

"And there's no such company?" Carter asked.

"Afraid not," Garfield sighed. "And within twenty minutes after you pulled out, Nick, they vanished. Not a trace."

Carter picked up another photo from the stack on the desk. This one he hadn't taken. It was a shot of Rafael Oheda floating face-up in the bay.

"Whoever Rubber Mask is, he doesn't leave anything dangling, does he."

Jillian moved back to the desk. "The rebels in Luzon will still be wanting what this guy has to sell. Ten to one they'll send someone else to deal. Shall I go back to Manila and start at square one?"

Garfield spread his arms. "No word from Washington yet on either one of you." He stood and started gathering the photographs and reports into his briefcase. "The safe house, the pool, and the booze are yours for as long as you're here. Both of you might as well enjoy it all, make a holiday of it."

Carter drifted to the huge window that overlooked Kowloon and Hong Kong harbor as Garfield moved toward the door.

"Dick?"

"Yeah?"

"What is this Toong Lu crap the one spouted?"

"It's some kind of Chinese cult. The research boys are working up a brief on it now. I'll get it to you as soon as I hear."

"One other thing . . ."

"Yeah?"

"Charlie Verrain," Carter said. When he got no response, he turned. "Well?"

"He's four days overdue, Nick. I'll keep you posted on that, too."

"Yeah," Carter said dryly, turning back to the window, "you do that."

He heard the door close behind Garfield, and a moment

later the sound of his car backing out the drive. He stood looking down at the sun-drenched city and the harbor for several moments in silence. When Jillian spoke, it surprised him. He had forgotten there was anyone in the room.

"Charlie Verrain? Friend of yours?"

"You know better than that. We don't have any friends in our business."

"Yeah, I know."

The dull sound in her voice made Carter turn. She was fixing yet another drink, and she wasn't doing it too steadily. Watching her, he remembered what she'd looked like in the swimsuit twenty-four hours before.

God, had it been only twenty-four hours?

She felt his eyes, and looked up. "Something?"

"Just wondering what you looked like nude."

She giggled. "Want to find out? Garfield told us to make a holiday out of it."

All the boredom of the days before the action and then the tenseness of the last twenty-four hours boiled to the surface at once.

He didn't wait. He swept her off her feet and into his arms, put his lips on hers, took her kisses. Her lips clung softly, giving him back kiss for kiss, and all the while he was moving as fast as he could to a bedroom.

He put her down and swiftly undressed her. The dress fastened down the front, and he had it off in no time. She wore a slip, bra, panties, and these he stripped away, with her help.

When he saw her nude, he sucked in his breath. She wasn't tall, and didn't weigh much over a hundred pounds. Her breasts were high and firm, the nipples stood erect. They were tan, and the area around them was tan, melting into the honeyed tan of her body.

Her waist was tiny; he spanned it with his two hands. Her shapely bottom was dimpled. Her upper thighs curved softly, cradling the brown, soft place of her womanhood, then flowed exquisitely from knees to perfect ankles and narrow feet.

He couldn't take time to kiss her again. He tore off his own clothes, ripping seams, but he didn't give a damn. By the time he was naked, she was on the bed, arms open.

Fiercely her hands cupped his face, pulling his mouth down to her parted lips in a hungry kiss.

Carter gave a low murmur of surprise, his muscular body pressing her farther into the bed, taking over control. His hard tongue probed the moist sweetness of her mouth, his hands slowly caressing the swelling curves of her breasts.

She sighed, nuzzling her cheek against his jaw. Her skin was warm and smelled of a spicy scent. Her body felt boneless beneath his exploring hands. His mind floated on a sea of pleasurable sensations, his own passion mounting with such a force that it made him tremble.

A soft moan of pleasure escaped her lips when Nick's mouth followed the curve of her swelling breasts, his beard-roughened cheek gently resting in the scented valley. His muscular thigh slid intimately between her legs.

The slow, sweet arousal of her body was an all-consuming flame that overrode her mind and made rational thinking impossible. Her heightened senses ached for complete possession, and with that came her final surrender.

"Make love to me, Nick," she whispered, her fingers lovingly tangled in the dark curly hairs of his chest.

Slowly they drew together, her head rolling to one side as his lips sought the rapidly beating pulse at the base of her throat. His mouth moved languidly over her neck, breathing in the haunting scent of her perfume before hungrily seeking the sweetness of her softly parted lips.

Her breasts shuddered under his hard tongue and skilled fingers, while her own hands caressed the muscles of his bare chest. Her trembling fingers followed the trail of hair down his stomach to lightly outline his navel.

She moaned with unconcealed desire when his lips sought the sensitive, hardened nipples of her full breasts.

"Now, please, now . . . I want to feel you inside me!" she groaned, and she grabbed for him with both hands, impatiently pulling him toward her and inside.

She ground against him hungrily as he thrust back and forth, filling her. He placed his hands under her buttocks, pulling her closer to him, and she moaned constantly from deep in her throat.

"More, more," she begged, and he gave her more.

The sweat was running down his body, and their bodies slid deliciously back and forth, glistening with heated perspiration. She matched his movements, side to side, then clockwise, then going the opposite way. He felt her inner self grip him, gasping as he sensed the blaze flash through her and envelop them both.

She began to quiver, slowly at first, then more, and more, and her body grew more desperate, thrusting harder and harder against him, faster and faster, every bit of her shaking.

She was gasping now, and he allowed himself full freedom, no longer trying to stop his own momentum, as the whole of the two of them meshed in one giant explosion, then broke up into individually shattering areas, as if each part of their bodies was having its own individual climax.

Slowly they subsided, panting, arms and legs still entwined around one another.

"Hey," Jillian said at last.

"Yeah?"

"Happy holiday!"

Carter awakened to the smell of coffee and noises somewhere in the house. He guessed the kitchen. It was dark outside the window, and the digital clock beside the bed read eight o'clock.

He sat up in the bed and smiled at the chaos: sheets and blankets half on, half off the bed, clothing flung in every direction, and even an overturned glass.

In the bathroom, he shaved and showered. When he reentered the bedroom, Jillian was waiting. She was carrying a tray and wearing nothing but a smile.

"Espresso. Care to drop your towel and join me?"

Carter chuckled and dropped the towel. He was halfway to her when the telephone rang.

"Yeah?"

"Nick, Dick Garfield. I'm glad I caught you before you went out to dinner. You're both on alert."

"Something pop?"

"Looks that way. Charlie Verrain. I'll be there in fifteen minutes."

The phone went dead. Carter hung up and turned to Jillian. "We'd better get dressed."

"We're back on?"

"Looks that way."

Garfield arrived in exactly fifteen minutes. He accepted a cup of espresso from Jillian and went right to work. He spread a new set of blowups across the coffee table.

"The film these were developed from came in a few hours ago from Leonard Markham. He's our consul general in Rangoon. It came in the pouch marked Eyes Only, for me."

"Verrain?" Carter asked, examining the pictures.

"No doubt about it. They originated with Charlie. But we've got a problem."

"What do you mean?"

"Markham sat on the package for three days. When it came in, there was a caustic little note with it to the effect that the gentlemen of the diplomatic corps don't appreciate playing mailmen for spooks."

"*What?*" Carter felt the flush hit his face.

Garfield shrugged. "Bureaucracy, Nick, you know how

it works. Markham owns a chain of fertilizer plants. He got his appointment because he contributed heavily to a particular campaign. In return he gets to play God for a few years."

"Bastard," Carter hissed. "Has Washington got a set of these?"

Garfield nodded. "Direct to Hawk. They're working on strategy now. That's why you're on a moment's standby."

"This looks like a ready-made shopping list from Oheda," Jillian said.

"Probably," Garfield agreed. "My hunch is that feelers are already going out to the Philippines for a new buyer. It's a sure bet the next one's going to be more cagey."

"Does that mean I head back to Manila?" she asked.

Garfield's face darkened. "I'm afraid not, Jillian. You're officially on a long holiday, somewhere quiet and away from the Far East."

Jillian's expression was grim. "It was me they spotted."

"Yeah. Word's out all over Southeast Asia. They've got a good description of you and they want you bad. My orders are to get you out and safe, tonight."

Jillian and Carter exchanged a quick look. It said: *Well, it was short and sweet, but it was fun while it lasted.*

"What have you got on this Sydney Chong?" Carter asked.

"He's big," Garfield replied. "Import-export, mostly valuable antiques. He's got a lot of clout and money, usually deals in whole collections."

Carter flipped one of the photos. "Quite a collection."

"He's got offices in Sydney, Singapore, and here in Hong Kong. He's also got a pretty strong pipeline into the Burmese government. Their laws are stringent, but Chong seems to be able to get anything he wants in or out of the country."

"You think Charlie Verrain was in Burma when he took these?"

"Hard to pinpoint," Garfield replied, "but we think he was, yes. The last tag we got from him is MI6 in Bangkok.

They loaned him a Land-Rover and pushed a visa for Burma through for him."

"Any way of substantiating if Charlie used the visa?" Jillian asked.

Garfield chuckled dryly. "If our satellites said it was monsoon in Burma and we asked them the rainfall, they'd tell us they're in the middle of a drought."

"This could be tough," Carter growled.

"No doubt about it. Washington's doing prelims now, trying to find a way to get you in."

"Anything at all on Charlie?"

"Nothing, not even a shoelace. Even the Rover has disappeared."

"Jesus," Carter hissed, and moved to the bar. He needed scotch, not espresso.

"Jillian," Garfield said, "you'd better pack."

"Now? You mean you want me to leave with you right now?" she exclaimed.

He looked from one to the other, and shrugged. "I'll have a car pick you up in an hour. Be ready."

"Yeah."

Garfield left, leaving an awkward silence behind him.

Finally, Jillian stood and moved toward her bedroom. "I'd better pack."

"Yeah," Carter said, refilling his glass.

He handled it for a couple of minutes, downed the drink, and walked into the bedroom.

There were no words.

He turned her toward him and looked down at her lips. They were slightly parted, lush and full, still rich with promise. Her lids half closed as she looked up at him. The desire was in her eyes more than ever, and he could feel her breath deepen as he bent down to kiss her.

Her lips responded as he placed his own lightly on them, and then more firmly. He felt her body tense, and then relax as she gave herself up. He pulled his head back and stared down at her, and her mouth was slightly open, glistening teeth showing, as if every last bit of her were hungry for more.

He obliged her desire, kissing her again, feeling as if he had been drawn into a whirlpool, sinking more and more deeply into the vortex of her passion. His strong hands began to caress her back, working up and down, each stroke bringing an accompanying sigh from her.

His hand was under her blouse now, running up along the spine, reveling in the velvet of her skin, stroking, massaging, pressing her closer to him. He could feel the beating of her heart, rapid and urgent.

He pushed her gently away from him and deftly undid the clasp of her bra. In her excitement she seemed almost not to see him, lost in her sensuality. Slowly he unbuttoned the front of her blouse, until it fell open, exposing her breasts, tan nipples erect.

He removed the blouse and drew her back to him, running his hands over her as they kissed, their tongues working feverishly together.

"I want you," she breathed, barely able to get out the words.

"I want you," he answered, and lifted her to the bed. Her body trembled against him. "We have fifty-five minutes," he growled, his voice husky with desire.

"Then let's not waste a second."

SIX

The rain was more of a bother than anything else. It came down in tiny droplets that seemed to have a great deal of space between them. Like any summer rain, it seemed warm until it seeped under your collar and ran down your back. It was a typical London rain.

And it was bothering the tall, long-limbed woman in the dark raincoat. Under her breath she cursed the fact that she had to be out in it at all. If Queen and Country were calling her, why couldn't they call her in the dry warmth of her flat?

She skirted the Knightsbridge side of the Serpentine, and, walking along the water's edge, turned into the wind blowing over Hyde Park. As she approached a landing stage for the rowboat rentals, a tall, aristocratic man stepped from the shadows holding an umbrella. He moved forward and fell into step beside the woman.

"Nasty night. Miss Camway? . . .Francine Camway?"

"You bloody well know who I am. Who the hell are you?"

The man rolled his eyes her way and pursed his lips. He was not short, but even in low, sensible heels she towered four inches above him. Under his hat she saw gray hair,

59

and his clothing was tailored, probably Savile Row.

"My name is Jonathan Hart-Davis. My credentials."

He passed a plastic-encased card to her just as they passed under a streetlight. The photo on the card matched his face, and Her Majesty's seal was in the upper right-hand corner. His job designation was printed across the card in dark blue ink.

"All right, you're MI6, and I'm properly impressed." She handed the card back. "What do you want with me?"

"It would seem that you have a particular job skill that we are in desperate need of, Miss Camway."

She stopped and turned to face him directly. The brim of her hat lifted to reveal a fine-boned, cool face, made almost mysterious by slanting eyes of a pale green color that flashed almost opalescent when the light hit them just right, their eyebrows thinly arched below a high, pale brow. Her ash-blond hair was drawn back from her face and held in a plastic barrette at the nape of her neck.

"What does MI6 want with a secondary member of the British Museum's Far East division?"

Hart-Davis chuckled. "You underrate yourself, Miss Camway. You are the leading expert on Southeast Asian antiquities."

She shrugged and water leaped from the shoulders of her raincoat. "I've got some questions."

"There's a bench that looks fairly dry," he replied, taking her arm. "Shall we sit?"

"I'd rather sit in that pub over there. I'm well to freezing my bum off."

"Amazing," Hart-Davis chuckled. "You have more degrees than a thermometer and you talk like a Soho tart."

"I had humble beginnings," she retorted. "What about the pub?"

He sighed. "Impossible, I'm afraid. I really can't be seen in public with you, especially once you agree to take part in a little project of ours."

"Once I agree?" she said, bristling. "You've got a bloody nerve . . ."

"Yes, I do," he said with a grin. "It comes with the business, I'm afraid. Please, sit down. There, that's better." Suddenly there was a rough harshness about his voice, as if his throat were dry. "Now, to, um, business, as it were. Does the name Sydney Chong mean anything to you?"

She concentrated. "Vaguely. Is he a collector?"

Hart-Davis nodded and said dryly, "Among other things. Sydney Chong has the largest known collection of antiquities from the Yuan, or Mongol, dynasty in China under Kublai Khan."

A light came on in her eyes. "Now I remember . . . Rangoon."

"That's right."

Her eyes narrowed in concentration. "Not a truly valuable collection, as I remember, and not completely authenticated."

"The collection really doesn't interest us, Miss Camway. Sydney Chong and his other interests do."

"Such as?"

"Miss Camway, I must warn you that, whether or not you agree to help us, what I am about to tell you must never be repeated to another soul."

"Fair enough."

"When the Americans left Vietnam, they left behind them millions and millions of dollars' worth of military hardware. A lot of it has become outdated, of course, but it is still dangerous and effective. Hanoi needs hard cash. We believe they are raising it by selling those arms to rebel insurgents in Third World countries. And we suspect that Sydney Chong is their broker."

She nodded. "All right, I follow you so far.

"We would like to send a team into Rangoon, specifically into the village of Kamwaddy, where Chong has converted a pair of old mansions into a museum and warehouse."

"A team . . . ?"

"Yes. You, representing the British Museum, and an American, ostensibly from the Metropolitan Museum in New York. We have already made a request of Chong, in the name of the British Museum, for a showing of his antiquities here in London some time next year. We have every reason to expect that the request will be granted."

" 'Ostensibly' is a big word."

Hart-Davis smiled. "Actually, the American is a top agent. Under cover of your work, we hope he can unmask Sydney Chong and stop the pipeline."

She shook her head firmly. "I'm afraid you've got the wrong person. Not only do I not agree with what you people do, but I'm also a coward. If this Sydney Chong is what you think he is, I don't think he'll take kindly to someone poking around in his deals."

"Quite right," Hart-Davis replied in a whisper. "The Americans have already lost one agent who was, as you say, poking around."

"That puts a lid on it, then," she said, rising. "Nice meeting you, Mr. Hart-Davis. Give my regards to the Queen." She started away.

"Miss Camway . . ."

"What?" she said over her shoulder, still moving.

"I believe you are about to be given a very large grant for an upcoming dig in the Celebes . . . around Đanau Poso, to be exact."

She slowed. "That's right."

"And I believe your appointment at the museum comes up for review next year."

She stopped, hunched her shoulders, and whirled. "You wouldn't dare."

Hart-Davis smiled almost sadly. "I'm afraid, Miss Camway, that I would."

"The grant, maybe, but you can't touch my job. You haven't *that* kind of power!"

"As sad as you may think it is, I have that much power . . . and more."

"You son of a bitch, you bastard, you bloody pompous ass—"

"Miss Camway, I assure you—"

"Fuck you!" She whirled and stalked away in the rain.

Hart-Davis retrieved a cigarette case from his inner pocket. He tapped a Players and placed it between his lips. After a few drags he heard the tapping of her heels to his right. She had made a wide swing around him.

"With bastards like you, how did we ever lose the Empire!" She sat, stiffly. "Give me a bloody cigarette."

He did, and lit it for her. "You will be more than adequately compensated."

"That's great," she replied, inhaling deeply. "Who will I leave it to, my bloody ex-husband?"

"The man you'll be going in with is an expert, with years of experience. Believe me, he's the very best. He has been instructed that only one thing is to supercede the success of the mission, and that is your safety."

She snorted. "That makes me feel ever so good. God, I hate you bloody spooks!" Another long drag on the cigarette, then a deep sigh. "All right, what do I do?"

"I believe you've applied for a week's holiday?"

"That's right, to Tenerife."

"Fine, take it, starting Monday. Only you won't be going to Tenerife.

"No?"

"No, you'll be going to southern Portugal. We have rented a villa there for you and the American. You'll be posing as a married couple, Mr. and Mrs. Young . . ."

She whirled on him. "I thought I was going into Burma! Now you want me to use my holiday to shack up with a bloody American spook?"

Hart-Davis continued as if she hadn't spoken. "His name is Nick Carter. In that week, you must give him a crash course in your field. He will have to be able to convince Sydney Chong that he is an expert."

"Impossible!"

"In our business, Miss Camway, nothing is impossible. Here is an air ticket in the name of Francine Young. Also a passport and all the other documentation you will need. Also a thousand pounds for spending money . . ."

"You bastard. You bloody well knew that you could force me into doing this, didn't you!"

"Miss Camway, for an intellectual, you have a remarkably limited vocabulary. I suggest you pack swimming gear. The Algarve is lovely this time of year. Good evening."

He pulled up the collar of his raincoat and moved away in the direction of Hyde Park Corner. She watched until he was lost in the rain. Only then did she begin to walk at a brisk pace in the opposite direction.

Bonkers! I've gone bloody bonkers! she muttered to herself.

SEVEN

She was easy to spot, moving like a thoroughbred toward the baggage claim of the Faro airport. She was tall, a head taller than the other passengers, her ash-blond hair flowing casually beneath a wide, floppy hat. She wore a simple summery dress, the green color of the Mediterranean under a bright sun. Her eyes, brooding, almost matched the dress.

Carter waited until she had paused a little way from the others near the conveyer belt, and then moved forward.

"Franny, darling!" He tugged her into his arms and planted his lips to hers before she could avert her face. He made the kiss just husbandly enough, and then retained the hug with his lips close to her ear, partially hidden by her hair.

"I assume you're Carter," she whispered.

"I am."

"Was that necessary?"

"It was. You forgot your wedding band."

"I tried to put on my old one before I got on the plane, but I couldn't. It made me throw up."

Ah, fun, Carter thought. *This is going to be real fun!*

But then Hart-Davis had said that Francine Camway might

65

be a tad difficult. Already, Carter was guessing that a *tad* was a tad of an understatement.

He broke the clinch. "Which bags did you bring, dear? The tan Guccis?"

"No," she replied dryly, "the canvas Marks and Spencers."

Carter couldn't suppress a smile. This one would be a bitch to win over, but he felt there would be something there if he could manage it.

There was something intangible about her. Even with the barely concealed anger, she was beautiful, the way a painting one doesn't quite understand is beautiful.

It was the eyes, he decided, the way her high and wide-spaced cheekbones made those big green eyes even bigger.

"Did you miss me?"

"Loads, *darling*." The smile had a bit of acid in it and drew her skin taut.

"How was the flight?"

"Bumpy. There they are."

Carter grabbed the two bags. One of them lengthened his right arm a few inches. "Heavy."

"Books. I was told you needed some educating."

He matched her smile. "We'll both get some educating before this is over. Shall we go? The car is this way."

Carter pressed his right foot almost to the floor just outside Faro. It was a beautiful day on the Algarve, with rolling farmland on their right and tall, majestic cliffs down to the sea on their left.

"The villa overlooks the sea from a cliff just south of Praia da Rocha. I think you'll like it." His vibrant voice rose easily above the whoosh of air that skimmed the sides of the sports car. He managed what he hoped was a relaxed grin as he threw a glance her way.

"Do I have my own bedroom?" She spoke facing directly front.

"There are four bedrooms. I haven't unpacked yet, so you can take your pick."

"That's some consolation."

She was holding the floppy hat down against the grasp of the wind. Beneath it, her hair blew in disarray around her shoulders.

"I've laid out a basic itinerary for us."

"Oh?"

"Yeah. Book learning and lectures from you in the mornings, physical training and small arms from me in the afternoon. We'll start tomorrow."

"Guns?" she cried. "I hate guns!"

"So do I, but they might come in just as handy as your books."

"The bloke in London said all that was required of me was my scholarly expertise!"

Carter nodded and pushed the Ferrari to a whine as he passed a line of trucks. "I'm afraid Jonathan might have bent it a little there."

"Swell. What kind of physical training?"

"How far can you run without resting?"

"From the bar to the loo," she quipped.

"A week from now, you'll be doing five miles easy."

"The bloody hell I will."

Carter grinned, broadly.

They didn't speak the rest of the way to the villa.

It was perched on one of the lower cliffs, directly above the ocean. Patterns of sun and shade defined the low, rambling walls, and flowering vines crept up trellises and softened the geometry of the Moorish architecture.

Carter stopped the car in front of the entrance. Beyond the curving drive, a fountain bubbled loudly in the silence.

He moved around to the rear and opened the trunk. Then he strolled toward the front door.

She stood beside the rear of the car. "Where are you going?"

"This is the villa," he replied.

"What about the bags?"

"What about them?" he said, opening the door and entering.

"Damn," she hissed, and struggled the bags from the trunk, following him through the door.

"I suggest you take the front bedroom on the second floor. It's by far the best view."

She dropped the book bag on the floor at his feet. "This one's yours."

He grinned. "I'll guard it with my life."

Her huge eyes avoided his glance as she headed for the stairs, her heels making the sound of .22-caliber pistol shots on the tile floor.

"Would you like a drink?"

"Yes! Gin!" she shouted over her shoulder, and disappeared into the room.

He grabbed his own bag and moved into the lower bedroom. He changed into swimming trunks, put on a short beach robe, and grabbed two towels. In one of them he rolled the loaded Luger.

At the bar, he fixed her drink and opened a beer for himself.

She was hanging clothes in the closet when he entered. "Your drink, madame."

"Thank you."

"Don't mention it."

She tipped the drink as she eased into an easy chair, and then noticed his dress. "What's this?"

"I told you we don't start until tomorrow. I'm going

swimming. Join me if you like." He moved to the door. "You are supposed to be on holiday, remember?"

She had the urge to throw the glass at him, but her conservative nature wouldn't let her waste good English gin.

The beach was a honey-colored, sugary stretch of land shaped like a horseshoe and enclosed on three sides by tall, craggy sandstone cliffs. It looked inaccessible to the casual eye, but workmen had chiseled a stairway hewn out of the rock down to the shore. It was a steep, winding trail, and not many people used the beach for that reason, so it was quiet and secluded.

He had been on the beach only about twenty minutes when she appeared. She stopped about ten feet from him and spread a towel. She dropped a second towel, and shrugged out of a short terry robe.

She wore a bikini beneath it, just enough to cover the essentials. Her breasts were small but firm, her belly flat, her thighs and hips just fleshy enough, and her legs were long, long, long.

"You've got a beautiful figure."

She glanced his way, all prepared for a haughty reply. Then her eyes narrowed as they took in his lean, muscular body with the purple and white scars gleaming like lines in a road map through his tan.

"My God . . ."

He grinned. "That's usually everyone's reaction."

"How . . ."

"I didn't get 'em falling off a bicycle." He put his head back down on the rolled towel.

She shook her own head and went into the ocean. Now and then Carter opened his eyes to watch her swim or bound in and out of the sea. She was enjoying herself. Good, he thought, the ice was going to have to melt fairly fast; they didn't have a hell of a lot of time.

She cavorted for about a half hour, and then returned to her towels and robe.

"I have a suggestion."

"What's that?" she asked.

"That you move over closer to me. Whether you like it or not, we're going to have to start acting like the loving married couple in public."

She hesitated, but eventually moved her gear closer and dropped to her knees beside him. Everything moved nicely as she worked the towel over her body.

Carter averted his eyes from her sleek lines, studying instead the long expanse of beach and blue water, and the caves dug out of the cliffs by the pounding surf.

"This Sydney Chong character . . ."

"Yeah?" Carter said, shielding his eyes with a forearm.

"What happens if you find out that he is brokering all this military hardware?"

"I put him out of business."

She rolled to an elbow. One rosy nipple peeked from above her bra. She didn't seem to notice. "Just like that?"

Carter reopened one eye and peered through his fingers at her. "Just like that."

She studied him for a long minute. "How?"

He got to his feet. "You don't want to know that." He trotted down to the water and dived in.

He swam out to one corner of the horseshoe, across the opening to the other, and back to the beach. When he got back to where she sat, he sensed the strange look in her eyes. She held out his towel.

"I unfolded your towel for you." She shifted slightly and Carter saw the Luger sitting beside her. "I guess now I know how."

•   •   •

Kublai Khan was the son of Tului and the grandson of old Genghis. In 1252 he moved into China and started conquering the hell out of things. By 1260 he had expelled the Kin Tartars and founded the Mongol dynasty. He treated the conquered humanely, unlike his forebears, and built the city of Khanbalik, which became Beijing.

Kublai Khan was a patron of literature and the arts. He commissioned paintings, books, vast Buddhist scrolls and artworks. Many Yuan-style religious sculptures in miniature survived, and most of them were in the Sydney Chong collection.

Carter learned to identify these by sight, and he was soon able to distinguish the real from the fake.

Francine Camway knew her subject well and had the ability to pass the information on in digestible lumps.

The assignment also proved easier than she had anticipated. Carter had an extremely quick and agile mind. He was able to absorb, memorize, and parrot back vast amounts of information in unbelievably short periods of time. All this while equating the material's value.

She commented on it in undisguised amazement.

"It's not as great as you think," he replied offhandedly. "It's a trick, really. Actually, it's been trained into me, part of the business."

She accepted it as such, but it still did wonders for her ego to think she could teach him so quickly.

All this was in the mornings. The afternoons were a different story.

For all of her negative remarks, Francine Camway had in fact been an outdoors person much of her life. She thought nothing of walking great distances, and she was an accomplished horsewoman and tennis player.

But nothing had prepared her for what Carter put her through.

The exercises were for speed and agility. "Strength means nothing," he told her. "With the right knowledge, the speed, and the body control, a ten-year-old girl of eighty pounds could kill a six-foot man with her bare fingers."

Francine Camway had no intention of killing anyone with her bare fingers, but she was too weary to argue. Also, Carter had a way of goading her into matching what he delivered.

He was scoring A-plus on his studies. Why couldn't she do as much on hers?

He concentrated on building her stamina with exercise and long runs. By the fourth day, she had learned the pressure points of the body well enough that, had Carter not been the instructor, she could have taken him down.

Since Verrain's photos showed American M-16s in the crates, he schooled her on loading and firing that rifle, as well as his Luger.

"If it comes to it, you'll just have to have a good eye. We wouldn't dare use a range, even if we could find one around here."

So they were restricted to gun training with only dry firing. But Carter could tell that she would have a good eye. The question was, would she use it and fire on a man to kill if she had to?

The morning of the fifth day, Carter breezed through the three-hundred-question quiz Francine had prepared, missing only one item.

That afternoon she made five miles on the run with no stops, and managed to drop Carter with a blind head chop after a clever foot feint.

"Congratulations," he said with a laugh, shaking the sudden cobwebs from his head. "It's time for a little R and R tonight."

"Oh?"

"Yeah, dinner out."

"Thank God. Your cooking is lousy."

He shrugged. "The same as yours."

She laughed, the first since they had arrived. "I know. I don't think either one of us is very domestic."

Carter chose a little Dutch-owned restaurant in the village of Carvoeiro that sat on a cliff. It was idyllic, with excellent food, a view of both the village and the moonlit sea, and a small string band for dancing.

Much to his surprise, midway through the meal Francine got curious.

"How long have you . . . been doing what you do?"

"A long time," he replied after a moment. "Maybe too long."

She tried to find out where he was from, what kind of a boyhood he'd had, what had brought him into such work.

He evaded, skillfully, but enough. He turned the questions back on her, on purpose. To his further surprise, she rattled on as if she was sure he would want to know all about her, which, in fact, he did not.

She had been born in Liverpool, illegitimate. Her mother had likewise been born illegitimate. She made sure that Francine got an education, and within weeks of Francine's graduation, her mother had died.

"I guess that's why I took up the past as an interest. The future always looked so bloody bleak."

"More wine?"

"Yeah, sure. You ever been married?"

"No," Carter replied, "I never stopped long enough in one place."

"I did, twice. God, that was bloody balls-up. The first one was a drunk. The second one wanted a mother. Who needed it? Cheers!"

They drank and danced and the evening got mellow.

Four boisterous Germans had moved in a few tables away just as Carter and Francine had finished their meal. Since Francine was the only woman in the place—married or not, they didn't seem to care—two of them had oozed over to the table and asked her to dance.

Politely but sternly, Francine had refused.

Now they were all four boisterously drunk. So much so that conversation was out of the question.

"Had enough?" Carter asked at last.

"Yeah. Bloody schoolboys at their age. I'll go to the loo and meet you at the door."

Carter was in the foyer. He had just completed paying the check and making the tip, when all hell broke loose in the dining room.

He ran back in, with the owner at his heels. One look told him everything.

One of the Germans had apparently tried one last time with Francine, and when she again turned him down he had insisted.

He was now on the floor, out cold. Carter could see his foot already swelling around his shoe where she had used her heel on his instep, and by morning the whole left side of his face would be blue.

His three pals were holding to their table, their mouths open like a trio of baby birds.

"Any problem?"

"Hell, no," she chuckled. "Let's go home."

She got even better by the end of the seven-day period.

Both of them were ready to go, but the phone never rang.

Neither of them let up on the eighth or ninth day. Both of those evenings, they went out to dinner instead of cooking in. It was by mutual consent. The time, working together in the kitchen, eating, and then cleaning up, put them in too much contact.

The next day, Carter called a day off. Francine took to the beach and he drove to Lisbon. For an hour he went over what they had on the project, making sure that when the go came from Washington, everything would be ready.

"But still no word?"

"Nothing, Nick. I'll ring you down there the minute I hear."

He got back to the villa around eight. The sun was just dipping over the Atlantic when he parked and hit the front door.

The aroma that greeted him was delicious, and she was wearing an apron draped over a tight-fitting black dress that was cut deep between her breasts.

"What's this?"

"Hi, there," she said, grinning. "I thought you might like some wine with your dinner. I have red or white . . . which would you prefer?"

"Both. You cooked?"

"No, I had it catered. It's edible." She forced a hurt look, but her eyes betrayed the mirth.

Carter looked at her with new respect. She was the same woman as before, only now there were subtle differences. Instead of appearing hard and brazen, she now seemed soft and vulnerable. Her long hair was tied in a ponytail and hung softly over one shoulder. Her face was devoid of makeup except for a hint of lipstick. The dress clung to and emphasized every contour of her body. She sat on the sofa directly across from him, her legs tucked sideways beneath her. Cradled in each arm was a bottle of wine.

"What's the occasion?"

"Our anniversary, for God's sake. Ten days. Does there

have to be an occasion for me to go to all the trouble of ordering in?"

Carter laughed. "I'll wash up."

He had to pass her to reach the door to the next room. She stood, and he caught the smell of her perfume, faint and musky. He closed the door, then stopped and stood motionless. Every muscle in his body was tense and his mind was in a turmoil. He waited until the tension eased away.

No good, he thought, *not with this one.* Jillian Sorbonnia was different. She was in the business and she knew nothing would last.

But this one, she was talking tough, but under all that beautiful skin she was a romantic.

She was placing two wineglasses on the table when Carter returned. She looked up and smiled as if enjoying the role of hostess. All traces of her previous mood had vanished. Perhaps she, too, had done some soul-searching.

"It looks good," he said, eyeing the table.

"It certainly does," she replied, "and I'm ravenous! Now, what kind of wine will we have? They're both local and I've never heard of either of them before." She held out the bottles, labels up. He pointed at one. The corks had already been loosened. He accepted one of the glasses and they toasted.

"To Kublai Khan," he said.

"To maybe all spooks ain't so bad after all," she said.

The meal was delicious and the conversation was neutral. When all the wine except two glasses had disappeared, they moved together to do the kitchen number.

It happened over the dishwasher. They were both closing the lid. Their hands came together and she seemed to glide into his arms. He was about to kiss her, when the telephone killed the mood.

He answered it. He mostly listened, now and then grunting a reply. Then he hung up and turned.

"It's on. We fly out of Lisbon tomorrow morning."

"Well," she shrugged, "it's been a hell of a holiday."

Yeah, Carter thought. Where had he heard that before?

Without any more conversation, they moved to their respective bedrooms and closed the doors behind them.

EIGHT

It was pouring, a wall of water, as the Thai International flight from Bangkok dropped onto the deck at Rangoon's Mingaladon Airport.

The moment they deplaned, the tight bureaucracy of the government reared its ugly head. They went through customs at a snail's pace, literally declaring everything in their bags, their pockets, and their wallets. Both of them were questioned endlessly about their special visas granting them unlimited time in Burma beyond the usual tourist limit of seven days.

After nearly two hours of bickering and assuring four echelons of minor officials that they hadn't obtained their long-term visas in order to overthrow the country, they were given their bags.

In the large, hot main room of the terminal, a tall Chinese with a stocky body and a shaved head approached as they exited the door from customs. A cardboard sign across his chest read: MISS CAMWAY, MR. ELLISON.

Frederick Ellison was in the Far East Asian Studies department of Columbia University; his specialty was antiquities. At the moment he was sunning himself in the Canary Islands at U.S. government expense.

"I am Ellison. This is Miss Camway," Carter said in Mandarin.

"I am Johnny Po, driver for Sydney Chong. I am to take you to Strand Hotel."

There were four bags, all heavy. He stuffed them under his arms as if they were lightweight packages, and took off.

"Pleasant bloke, isn't he?" Francine whispered.

"I don't think he gets paid to be pleasant," Carter replied. He didn't add that he had spotted a small revolver in an ankle rig under the man's trousers.

The car was a Mercedes limousine, not new, but years younger than the ancient taxi and few private vehicles on the street.

On the twelve-mile drive into the city, Johnny Po wasn't too talkative. Carter asked him a few questions about when they could expect to see Mr. Chong, and if there would be any problem about housing in Kamwaddy.

He got no reply.

Finally, Carter sat back and counted pagodas during the ride.

Francine was in her element. With each turn she got more excited. The peak was when they passed the huge Shwe Dagon Pagoda, with its 326-foot spire all covered in gold.

"Real gold," she murmured. "Eight thousand six hundred eighty-eight square-foot sheets."

Carter nodded and dropped his eyes to the filth and poverty of the streets. *At $12,000 a sheet,* he thought, *8,688 sheets of gold would buy one hell of a lot of rice.*

They hit the river, turned right, and pulled up in front of the Strand Hotel. In no time, Johnny Po had the bags out of the trunk. He dropped them onto the sidewalk and turned to Carter.

"Here, six tomorrow morning. I drive you to Kamwaddy.

Good day." He climbed back into the limo and drove off.

A bellman grabbed their luggage. Just inside the lobby, Carter fell back and returned to the revolving doors. A little less than a block down the street, he saw the limousine pull up beside a dark green Honda with two men in the front seat.

Johnny Po rolled down the electric window on the passenger side. He and the driver of the Honda exchanged a few words and nods, and the limo took off again.

Carter moved on across the lobby.

"Something wrong?" Francine asked.

"Maybe . . . maybe not."

They checked in and found out that their rooms were not adjacent. They were not even on the same floor.

Two bellmen escorted them in the elevator. At four, Francine stepped off.

"Dinner in about an hour?" Carter asked.

"Make it two," she replied. "I want a long hot bath."

The elevator went on up to six. They entered Carter's room and the bellman ran around doing the same things bellmen do all over the world. This was to give you time to get out your wallet and figure a tip.

When he was gone, Carter moved to the front window and carefully parted the curtain. The Honda was still there, but it had turned around and was now parked on the opposite side of the street facing the hotel entrance. The driver was leaning forward, staring up through the windshield.

Carter stared long and hard at the face until it was in his mind, and then took the elevator back down to the lobby.

The bar was doing a brisk business, although it wasn't too crowded. Carter had seen only the back of the passenger in the Honda, but it was enough. The man had been wearing a pink shirt and a little of the collar had shown above a dark jacket.

He was at the end of the bar, right by a glass window

that looked out onto the lobby. From his perch the man could also see the guest and service elevators.

He didn't even glance at Carter when he entered, but as the Killmaster moved on down to the other end of the bar he could feel the man's eyes boring into his back.

Carter ordered a drink and sipped it slowly while looking around the room. There were a couple of pretty women with a couple of ugly men, a table full of business types, and two more at the bar.

When Carter was sure that he had filed away that one's face, too, he finished his drink and returned to his room.

He showered, shaved, and called the desk to leave a wake-up call for seven. Then he lay down, naked, on the bed and dropped off at once.

At five minutes to eight he called down to Francine's room. "Dinner?"

"Lovely, I'm famished. Meet you in the lobby?"

"No, I'll stop by your room. There's a little something I have to do."

In the bathroom, Carter dug into his shaving kit. He removed the smaller of two shaving cream dispensers, and carefully sprayed the edges of drawers, the area around the closet door, and the opening to his briefcase and bag. This done, he lightly went over the whole with a towel. What appeared to be shaving cream disappeared to the eye and touch.

In the hall, he did the same thing around the edges of the door, and then took the elevator to the fourth floor.

Francine answered the door in something shimmery blue, with a tight bodice and cap sleeves. The skirt flared and fell gracefully in folds from her nice hips to just below her knees.

Carter stepped through the door and closed it behind him.

"Very nice," he said, letting his eyes travel all the way down and back up.

She flushed. "What's the 'little something' you have to do?"

"You'll see." He repeated the same performance on her doors, drawers, and bags that he had just finished in his own room.

"What's that stuff?"

"The chemical name is about as long as your arm. In the trade, we call it Sherlock Holmes dust."

"I don't get it . . ."

"You will." From the card case in his wallet, he took an ordinary credit card. He rubbed one end of it vigorously until it warmed, and then peeled it apart. From between the two layers of plastic, he withdrew a piece of pink gelatin. "This is ordinary theatrical gel, the kind they put over lights in theaters."

"Yeah?"

"Look." He ran the gel over the rim of her bag.

"That stuff you put on there glows . . . pink!"

"Right." He opened her bag, then closed it again. "Now look."

"Smudges. There are dark smudges in the color."

"Right again. If we have any visitors while we're gone, we'll know it. Let's eat!"

He paused on the sidewalk to light a cigarette. Out of the corner of his eye he spotted the Honda. There was only the driver. He hadn't noticed Pink Shirt in the bar, but it was ten to one he was already on his way up to their rooms.

"Something wrong?"

"Not really," Carter replied, "but I think we're about to be followed."

Her eyes grew wide and she gripped his arm a little tighter.

"Don't worry about it," he said. "My guess is that everybody who comes to Burma to see Sydney Chong is pretty well checked out before they get to him."

"Guilty or innocent?"

"Guilty or innocent," he answered. "Let's walk a bit and then take a cab."

They walked east along the strand and the river. After a few blocks, they turned left. At Merchant Street, Carter turned right and continued walking. The Honda was far back but it was there.

Satisfied, he stopped at the next cabstand.

"Are we?" Francine whispered as Carter handed her into the cab.

"We are, and, like I say, don't worry. It's all part of the game. Do you know the Café of Golden Dreams?" he asked the driver.

"Oh, yes, sir," the man replied. "Very nice place, good Burmese food."

The ride was about thirty minutes around Royal Lake and on north almost to the Turf Club. Twice, Carter had Francine fix her makeup. She didn't have to be told what for.

"Dark green Honda, four-door, one man."

"He's still there."

"Good," Carter said. "We want our man to know that we're as innocent as two lambs."

It was early in the week, so there was only a sprinkling of people at the tables. As was usual for Burma, few of them were tourists. Most looked like local middle-class couples and solo businessmen. Carter asked for a table near the stage and got it. At the rear of the small stage, a trio—including drums, piano, and the local version of guitar—played background music.

"You have entertainment, I believe?"

"Oh, yes, sir, very fine. A singer of Burmese songs."

Carter ordered drinks and the waiter left.

"You've been here before?" Francine asked.

"No," Carter said, and smiled. "I just like to be entertained. Our friend just arrived."

"Who?"

"The driver of the Honda. Don't look—he's sitting at the bar."

Carter ordered bird's nest soup, suckling pig, assorted dishes of curry, and lots of rice. Francine nodded, and Carter ordered a second drink. The man at the bar was watching them in the back-bar mirror, but Carter paid him no attention and kept up an animated conversation, mostly pumping Francine for yet more information about old Kublai and his antiquities.

The food came, and both of them fell on it like vultures. From then on there was little talk until the plates were taken away and tea was served.

Then a great gong sounded, and a woman appeared on stage in a narrow blue spotlight. She was tall for a Burmese, with straight black hair down to her shoulders, and the kind of dark beauty and full figure that oozes an aura of mystery.

She wore the traditional *ingyi* blouse, white and transparent, with a multicolored sarong skirt.

As the combo played behind her, she did a patter with the audience in a mixture of Burmese, Chinese, and English. She welcomed all the foreigners in the crowd, asking each of them in turn to raise their hands.

A young couple across the room were from England, and when she asked if there was anyone else from England, Carter told Francine to raise her hand.

"I hate this sort of thing . . ." she protested.

"Put your hand up," Carter ordered.

She did. Then the dark eyes on the stage strayed to Carter. "And you, sir?"

"U.S.A.," Carter said, grinning, "New York."

This went on for a minute or two longer, and then she sang.

She was good, and the combo backed her well. She sang a hot jazz number in English with a lot of soul, then an old blues melody in French. To everyone's surprise, she added a couple of numbers in Spanish and then a Portuguese fado.

Then she took a short talk break and played representative for the local tourist board.

"I hope many of our friends from abroad will be able to enrich their knowledge of our country while they are here. For instance, be sure to see the Kodagi Pagoda. It is very beautiful with its sixty-five-foot-tall statue of the Buddha. On the wall of the enclosure are over three hundred scenes in the events of the Buddha's life. Also, you must see the Botataung Pagoda. It was destroyed during World War Two, but it has been rebuilt and is very lovely . . ."

She rattled on for another couple of minutes, and then launched into a medley of native Burmese songs.

Carter signaled for the check.

"Hey, wait," Francine protested, "let's listen for a while."

"Can't," he replied. "Got an early morning, remember?"

"But . . ."

"Let's go, Fran."

Outside, he guided her into a cab. "Strand Hotel."

She moved against him. "What was all the rush?" she whispered.

"We got what we came for: sixty-five-foot statue, three hundred scenes, World War Two."

"Huh?"

"Six-three-two. It's a room number where we pick up our gear . . . the gear we couldn't bring into the country ourselves."

"You mean, the singer . . . ?"

Carter patted her arm. "We don't want to go into this with no backup, do we?"

He paid the cabdriver. They went to Francine's room first. There was a party down the hall and the door was open a crack, so Carter waited until they were inside before he took out the gel.

He could spot smudges everywhere they had looked. The room and baggage had been searched, and they had done a very thorough job of it.

"Bloody bastards! Makes my skin crawl," Francine gasped.

"It's not so bad when you know about it."

"The hell it isn't! I don't like anybody mucking about in my underwear!"

"Let's hope that's all they do," he quipped, brushing his lips across her cheek and heading for the door.

"You're leaving?"

"Got to collect our gear, remember?"

"Oh, yeah," she said, "room Six-thirty-two."

"See you at breakfast."

He took the elevator up to the sixth floor, smiling. Francine Camway had a pensive look on her face as he had closed the door. He wondered what she would do and say if he tapped on it in an hour.

He walked down the vacant hall to his own room, 659. There were smudges around the door. Inside, he found more, everywhere, and smiled.

Now that they had done a search and checked him and the woman out, it was unlikely that it would happen again. For the time being they would appear to be who they were supposed to be.

Carter retrieved a bottle of scotch from his bag, then took it with him into the hall. Ten seconds with a set of picks at the door of room 632, and he was inside. There was no one there, but there wasn't supposed to be anyone there.

In the closet was a bag identical to his own. It was empty.

He transferred everything, took the new bag, and checked the hall.

It was empty.

He hurried to his own room and let himself in. After making sure the door was locked and bolted securely, he took off his jacket and hung it up. Then he poured himself a scotch and sat down with the bag. There hadn't been time to let him know how it worked, so he had to go over it inch by inch and find out for himself.

There was a false bottom in the bag so cleverly made that there was no way to spot it, either in the shape of the bag or in its construction. There were several brass rivets around both the top and the bottom. He had already fooled with them, but on the second time around, it suddenly occurred to him to try something else. And that worked. The rivets on the bottom were all threaded, but it was a reverse thread, and they had to be turned to the right to loosen them.

A moment later he lifted out the false bottom. There, perfectly fitted in felt, was Wilhelmina, his 9mm Luger, a single-shot belt pistol, a broken-down Beretta machine pistol, and ten spare clips for the lot.

There was also a single page of Strand Hotel stationary. On it was scrawled a single Rangoon telephone number and the notation, "day or night."

Carter memorized the number and burned the paper. He rescrewed the false bottom into the bag and placed it in the closet.

He got out of his clothes and was about to crawl into bed, when, in the dimness, his eye fell across the telephone.

He started to reach for it, cursed himself, and fell into bed.

NINE

There was a brief respite from the rains of the monsoon on the early-morning drive to Kamwaddy. But the heat, when they reached the village and Johnny Po killed the air conditioner, was nearly unbearable.

The village was right out of the past, with only two buildings rising above one story and rice fields crawling right up to the four-block-long main street. The road was paved, up to the village. Then it was mud through the village and pavement again on the other side. It was as if the government was pissed off at the locals: "You want a modern road through your village, you build the damn thing!"

"Rustic," Carter muttered.

"Traditional," Francine replied.

The two buildings over one story were at opposite ends of the village. One was Government House, three stories, and the other was the hotel, also three stories.

Johnny Po parked just far enough from the old, cracked sidewalk so they had two good steps through the mud to get to it. When he stepped out, Carter could see that he had put on a pair of Wellington boots. He also had a smirk on his face.

This time Carter met him at the trunk of the Mercedes and hefted his own bag. It wouldn't do for Johnny Po to notice the vast difference in weight.

The next action was a repeat of the scene in front of the Strand in Rangoon. He dropped the bags and headed back for the car.

"When do we see Mr. Chong?" Francine asked.

"When he send for you."

And away he went, doing his best to throw mud at them from the spinning rear tires.

Between them they gathered the bags and entered the hotel lobby/bar. An emaciated little man in a white suit, an Errol Flynn mustache, and slicked-back, coal-black hair stood behind the bar. He studied them through droopy eyes from the door to the bar, and then managed an oily smile that didn't move the cigarette between his lips.

"Good afternoon," he said in English. "Welcome to Kamwaddy and my humble hotel. I am Sim Dok."

"Good afternoon," Carter nodded. "I am—"

"You want room?"

"Two rooms."

"Oh, you not married people?"

"No," Carter replied, barely concealing his anger.

"Not even girlfriend, boyfriend?"

Francine rolled her eyes. Carter shook his head.

"This is Francine Camway. I am Frederick Ellison."

"Oh, yes. You come see Mr. Chong. Sim Li!"

A pretty Burmese girl came through a set of beaded curtains, smiling. When she saw Carter, the smile disappeared and a sudden, guarded look came into her eyes.

"This Sim Li, my sister, very nice girl. She show lady her room. I take you."

"The rooms," Carter said, "will, of course, be side by side."

If Sim Dok had planned differently, the look in Carter's eyes and the tone of his voice changed the man's mind.

"Of course, side by side. This way."

Again they hefted their own bags and followed up the stairs to the third floor.

"Oh, sorry, not side by side, but right across hall . . . very easy to visit."

"The w.c.?" Francine asked.

"End of hall, very nice, very clean. My sister scrub every week. Have nice visit in Kamwaddy."

They minced down the stairs, leaving Carter and Francine in front of the open doors.

"Primitive," Carter grumbled.

"Traditional," she replied.

He smiled. "I'm glad you're so optimistic. Unpack, we'll case the territory."

The clouds, heavy-bellied with rain, were still threatening as they walked along the sea. In the distance, about a mile, they could see a huge pagodalike structure. It sat on the very edge of a cliff jutting out into the sea.

"Chong's?" Francine asked.

Carter nodded. "One of two. He lives in one, and the other is used for a museum and warehouse. The two are supposed to be close together. The other is probably on a lower level on the other side."

"Look!" She was pointing down into a cove about a hundred yards in front of them. A small ship was half-submerged just offshore, its superstructure and sides caked brown with rust. "I wonder how long that's been there?"

"Hard to say," Carter replied, "probably the thirties. Could have been an old Japanese or Chinese gunboat."

As they watched, they could see several urchins climbing along the superstructure, surefooted with their bare feet.

Several lines went out to sea.

"Tonight we'll probably be eating what they catch," Carter commented dryly.

They moved on, working their way along the undulating cliffs. The village had disappeared behind them when the wind suddenly picked up. They could see the young boys on the wreck dive into the water and swim for shore.

"I do believe it's coming," Carter said.

The words were scarcely out of his mouth when the wind began to roar and the rain came down.

"There's a hut there," he cried. "C'mon!"

They ran down the hill, but by the time they bolted through the doorless opening they were soaked. Just inside they paused, leaning against a wall so their eyes could adjust to the sudden dimness.

A sliver of light appeared in the ceiling and became a square opening. Then Carter noticed that a crude ladder led up to this trapdoor to the roof. A young boy, around fourteen, crept nimbly down the ladder. He wore nothing but bathing trunks, and looped around his neck, on a stringer, were four fish.

Then the Killmaster realized that this boy was one of the bunch they had seen on the wreck. He had come up over the opposite cliff, and instead of descending all the way on this side and walking back up to the hut, he had just entered through the roof.

He hit the dirt, went over to a far corner of the room—without seeing Carter and the woman by the front opening—and began building a fire in the blackened hearth.

Carter moved forward and spoke in Mandarin. "Hello. Sorry to invade your home, but the rain . . ."

The boy grinned up at him. Even with his dirt and grime he was a handsome teen-ager. "I know," he said, as if he always had strangers dropping in on him. "I see you running.

I guess you come here. Nowhere else to go except into sea. You and pretty lady want fish?"

Carter and Francine helped prepare the fish. As they did, Carter pumped the boy about the area, the village, and Sydney Chong. He got open answers to everything and everyone, except when it came to Sydney Chong. Here, the boy's face grew hard and his thin lips closed.

He would not speak of Sydney Chong.

Just as they were about to sit on the floor and eat from their laps, the boy crossed to a pile of rags in the opposite corner.

"Grandfather . . . Grandfather, fish."

The pile of rags stirred and an ancient face emerged. Deep wrinkles and shriveled cheeks rested serenely beneath sightless eyes.

The boy prepared a plate of fish and rice, and set it on the old man's lap. Immediately the fingers dug into the food on the plate and, like an automaton, brought the fish and rice to his toothless mouth.

The boy rejoined Carter and Francine. "My grandfather, he very old, blind."

They began eating, both Carter and Francine surprised at how hungry they suddenly were. The simple meal tasted delicious.

"Your parents don't live here with you?" Francine asked.

"My mother died," he replied, in such a way that the subject was closed.

From then on they ate in silence. When the meal was finished, the boy produced a bottle of rice wine. The three of them sat, sipping the wine. The old man had crawled back down into his rags.

The talk was general for almost an hour, and then, suddenly, the boy's face became animated, the eyes alive.

"I have beautiful sister. I show you picture."

He scampered to a chest in the corner of the room near the old man and came back with a framed photograph. Excitedly, he thrust it into Carter's hands.

"She May Won, very beautiful."

"Yes, she's very beautiful," Carter said, glancing at the photo and passing it to Francine.

She looked at it, then glanced up into Carter's eyes.

The woman in the photo was the same woman who had been the casino contact with Rafael Oheda. The same woman Carter had seen in the rear of the villa in Macao.

"What do you think?" she asked as they made their way up the rain-slick cliffs that would take them to the road and back to Kamwaddy. It was still raining, but it had slackened off to a drizzle and the wind had died down.

"I think the boy is starved for friendship."

"That was obvious. But if Sydney Chong is our man, and the boy's sister works for Chong . . ."

Carter shook his head. "There's more to it than that. You saw the way the boy clammed up when Chong's name was mentioned."

"And the hatred in his eyes," she added.

"While you label antiquities, I may go do a little fishing," Carter said. "Did you notice what that old man was sitting on underneath all those rags?"

"No."

"A bucket seat. And, unless I'm wrong, it had that horizontal tuck-and-roll pattern that only Land-Rover puts out."

Francine was about to reply, when suddenly three men emerged from behind scrub trees beside the road. There was little doubt of their intent as they circled. One of them had an enormous Webley, and the other two carried curved bolo knives.

The smallest of the three, the one with the Webley, came

straight toward them. The other two flanked.

"You have money?" the little man said in English. "American money, English money?"

There was something not quite right. Carter sensed it, and he also remembered who they were supposed to be. The two flankers were moving in too close. He could easily take one, and with the training he had given Francine, she could take the other one.

Even for petty or part-time muggers, these three were too careless to be real.

He glanced at Francine and saw what she was thinking. "Don't fight," he hissed under his breath. "I think that's just what they want us to do."

Suddenly the flanker on her side grabbed both of Francine's arms and ripped them up into the center of her back. Carter moved that way.

"Nick!" Francine cried. "Look out!"

Something exploded against the base of his skull, and white light danced a jig in front of his eyes. He lurched a step and went to his hands and knees in the mud. Bile in his throat made him gag.

He heard Francine cursing them and felt hands going through his pockets. There was a growl of pain and then a resounding slap.

"She bit my arm!" one of them howled. "The bitch took a piece out of my arm!"

"Did you get everything?"

"Yes."

"Then let's go."

Carter heard feet pounding in the mud, and then the sound of motorcycles.

He felt his head being lifted and then cradled. Soft, very soft breasts. He tried to open one eye. It wouldn't work. He gave up and passed out.

• • •

And then instead of black, there was white, a naked bulb hanging above him. Slowly a fractured face came together.

"Hi, Frannie," Carter said, tentatively reaching up to feel his head swathed in bandages.

"God, you must have a bloody thick skull. He hit you twice with the hilt of that awful knife, and the doctor says all you got is a bad bruise."

"Doctor . . . ?"

She nodded. "He looks like the village idiot, but he seems competent when he talks. He doesn't think you've got a concussion."

Carter blinked. "Where are we?"

"Back in the hotel. Can you see?"

"Vaguely. How did we get here?"

"The police arrived just a couple of minutes after the hooligans took off."

Carter smiled. It was painful, but he couldn't suppress it. "Figures."

"Oh? What's so funny?"

He glanced around. "We alone?"

"Yeah."

"Door shut?"

"Yeah."

"And locked?"

"Yeah."

"It figures," he said, "because the cops were probably waiting until those three got what they needed and then they moved in to do their duty."

Francine's eyes narrowed and she drew nearer, sitting in a chair beside the bed. "We were set up?"

He nodded, painfully. "I think so. Let me guess. They took your jewelry, your cash, your passport, and your visa."

"Righto," she said, "and I think that's what they got of

yours. We're supposed to go to the police at Government House in the morning and fill out some kind of complaint."

Again Carter nodded. "I'll do it, but it won't do any good. They won't be found until Sydney Chong wants them found."

"You mean . . . ?"

"Without passports and visas, it would be impossible to get out of the country. Hell, it would be tricky just moving around Burma."

Her face paled. "Then he knows."

"Don't think so," Carter replied. "He's just covering all bases. Sydney Chong doesn't miss a trick. Anybody he comes in contact with, he controls."

TEN

It was ten in the morning when Carter threw on a rain slicker and left the hotel. The rain had come up in sheets again, hard enough to obscure the ocean and, at times, the other end of the village. But the wind was light, allowing it to come straight down, so that by the time Carter entered Government House he was still relatively dry under the slicker.

There was a policeman at a desk just inside the door, sipping tea and looking bored. Carter identified himself and explained that he had been told to report and fill out a complaint. After he had said his piece three times—in English, Mandarin, and pidgin—the man's face lit up with understanding.

"Ah, that's Prefect Sin Chai. Second floor, first door on right." For him, that was apparently a lot of words. The moment he got them out, his lids drooped and his hand lurched for the teacup.

Carter moved up the stairs and turned right. He stopped at the first door and knocked. A voice growled something, and Carter entered. There was a single man sitting in a Spartan office.

"Come in, Mr. Ellison. Please, sit down. I am Sin Chai, Prefect of Police for Kamwaddy."

Carter stepped into the office, closed the door behind him, and took the proffered seat. He noticed that the man was inspecting him closely, so the Killmaster took advantage of the time to study him in return.

He was a short slender man, probably in his early forties. His uniform was immaculate, his black hair was slicked down and had a shine like patent leather. His face was thin and sharp, and there was a shrewd look in his eyes when he glanced up. It gave Carter the feeling that the man was gauging him, to see if the thieves had gotten all of his money.

"A most unfortunate incident last evening, Mr. Ellison," he said in only slightly accented English. "May I ask why you and Miss Camway were on the cliffs at that hour?"

Carter bit the inside of his lip to restrain his anger. From the man's tone, it was he and Francine who were the criminals. But it was no more than he had expected.

"It wasn't exactly a late hour, Prefect Sin. We had just been walking the cliffs during a letup in the rain, and we got caught."

"I see." The man glanced at a piece of paper on the desk. "Miss Camway reported to my men that your passports and visas were taken."

"That's right."

"It is a very bad thing to be in Burma without a passport and visa."

"I rather imagine," Carter said dryly. "Would you like a description of the three men?"

"Of course," he replied with a modest smile.

Carter gave him a detailed description. As he talked, Sin Chai made scrawling notes on a pad. Carter was sure the notes would never be transcribed, but went ahead with the farce. When he finished, Sin Chai tapped his pencil on the desk a few times, then seemed to make a decision.

"How is your injury?"

Carter shrugged. "A bad headache . . . I'll get over it."

"And Miss Camway?"

"Shaken, disturbed," Carter replied, "but not physically hurt."

"That is good." Here his face got extremely serious. "I want you to know, Mr. Ellison, that I and my staff will not stop until these men are apprehended and your property is returned to you."

Carter felt like screaming, but he managed to retain his composure. "I would appreciate that."

"In the meantime," Sin Chai continued, lighting a fresh cigarette from the burned-down butt, "I am afraid I must warn you not to travel outside the immediate area of Kamwaddy. Traveling without papers in Burma can be very dangerous. I'm sure you understand."

Carter was sure that if the man did a tongue-flicking number, the tongue would be forked. Again he managed to keep a solemn, straight face. "I understand perfectly, Prefect."

"Excellent. I wish you success with Mr. Chong. He is a fine man."

It was clearly a dismissal, which was fine with Carter. He had been in the office for only twenty minutes and he felt unclean.

He rose and walked to the door. "Thank you for your trouble, Prefect."

"No trouble, I assure you, Mr. Ellison. My duty."

Carter left. It was blatantly obvious to him that Prefect Sin Chai was in Sydney Chong's pocket.

Johnny Po and the limousine, with Francine in the rear,

was parked outside when Carter emerged.

"You go see Mr. Chong now?"

"A command performance," Carter said under his breath as he crawled into the car.

The house was gigantic, stucco and wood, mosaic and terra cotta, with angled traceries of fretted stone, twisting columns, and painted shutters. At the corners of the building rose little groups of towers, almost minaret-shaped and layered like a cake.

They drove through a wide portico and Johnny Po stopped the car.

"This way," he said.

Carter could see down the cliff. There was a marina at the base, well sheltered from the ocean. Five boats, ranging in size from a yacht to fishing skiffs, were moored there. Evidently, Sydney Chong liked to do a lot of sailing. Carter was fairly sure, from the excellent condition of the boats, that they didn't belong to any of the poverty-stricken fishermen in the area.

Then they were in a long hallway, a cavern of coolness from the oppressive humidity outside. They emerged from the hallway into a large foyer. A wide stairway spiraled upward to the top three floors.

Johnny Po started climbing, with Carter and Francine right behind him. What the Killmaster could see of the rooms through open doors looked like mini-warehouses. What little furniture there was, was sheet-covered.

It was obvious that Sydney Chong had an office in this monstrosity, and it was used for a warehouse. He hoped that other things besides antiquities were stored here.

Then they were in a long, thickly carpeted, rectangular room. A broad, uncurtained window looking out onto the

sea occupied the whole of one of the smaller walls. Before
it stood a flat-topped desk of black wood, its surface a pile
of papers, telexes, books, and a giant telephone setup.

Carter stood just inside the door as it closed behind Johnny
Po, and eyed the two occupants of the room.

A girl, for that was how she appeared now in a tight,
dark green *cheongsam*, sat on a divan some distance away.
She held a book in her hands, her body resting against the
cushions, slim and graceful with a quiet, contained insol-
ence. Her black hair was drawn back from her forehead,
and her eyes, dark and watchful, frankly examined Carter
and Francine, dismissed them, and returned to the book.

Carter's body relaxed. This was May Won and there had
been no sign of recognition in her eyes.

"Ah, Miss Camway . . ." The voice was deep and reson-
ant, the body tall and lean in an impeccable white suit, the
kind rich Southern plantation owners used to wear and gave
up eons ago. He advanced, bowed, and kissed Francine's
hand. "I am Sydney Chong."

"I am so happy to meet you at last, Mr. Chong."

"Sydney, please. And you would be Frederick Ellison."

Carter took the proffered hand. "How do you do?"

The small dark eyes, set deep under heavy brows, were
remote, alive, and observant. "I was appalled to hear of the
robbery. I must apologize for my countrymen."

"Aside from the loss of our passports and visas," Carter
replied smoothly, "I think it was mostly my dignity that
was bruised."

"Nevertheless, I have phoned the prefect and expressed
a personal concern that the scoundrels be found and
punished. Excuse me."

He turned and barked orders to the girl. Like a robot, she
nodded and fled the room. As she moved, the high slit of

her skirt parted enough for Carter to see a pair of very ugly bruises on her inner thigh.

"I have instructed May Won to see to our lunch. Until then, would you like to see the collection?"

"Very much," Francine replied.

Much to Carter's surprise and delight, she was playing Chong like a violin and he seemed to be enjoying it.

They went back down the expansive stairway to the third floor, and then through a series of rooms to the wing of the house away from the sea.

"I keep my private collections in this wing of the house on the second and third floors," Chong explained as they wound their way through the maze. "The first and fourth floors contain those things that I must buy and sell in order to live. Trade, as you scholars must realize, is a boring business, but necessary."

Carter hung back slightly as Francine and Chong jabbered. The man's English was Oxford, and his manners matched. The best word to describe him was smooth.

But there was something else, and the longer Carter studied him, the more he realized what it was. His walk was stealthy, a cross between a cat and a deer. Under the suit was a powerful, athletic body, and above his collar was a developed neck that would take a very hard blow before any damage could be done.

And, lastly, Carter could still feel the man's hand in his, the calloused side and heel of his palm and the two enlarged knuckles. Sydney Chong was a martial arts expert, and, Carter guessed, a deadly one.

Their passage through the various rooms was too quick for Carter to gain more than the swiftest impression of wealth and a certain bizarre taste. He glimpsed paintings and bronzes, faded brocade and dull gold on furniture, rich hangings and the soft glow of porcelain shining from wall and cabinet.

They moved through a low doorway into a wide storeroom lit by windows of frosted glass set into the thick walls. One side of the room was stacked with an assortment of heavy wooden cases covered with dust and straw. Some were stained with water, and most of them had parts of their sides rotted or ripped away.

"In those crates are the pieces of the Yüan dynasty collection that, as yet, have not been catalogued. The remainder of the collection is in wall cases on the floor below."

"I can't wait to begin," Francine sighed. "And you, Frederick?"

"The sooner the better," Carter replied, his face a mask of studied intellectualism.

"Excellent," Chong said, nodding. "Come, I'll show you the rest of the collection and then we'll have a bite to eat."

They returned to the stairway, and Carter suddenly stopped them. "Er, excuse me, Mr. Chong . . ."

"Sydney, please."

"Sydney, I wonder . . . the facilities?"

"Of course, that door on your right."

"Thank you," Carter said. "I'll join you on the second floor."

The two chatted their way down the stairs, and Carter darted into the w.c. He held the door open a crack until he could no longer hear their voices, and then padded as quietly and quickly as possible into the front wing of the house.

The place was enormous, with one long center hallway and two hallways off the main in each wing. Unlike the rooms in the inner wing, with their open or unlocked doors, the rooms in the outer wing were locked tight. And the locks weren't old, rusty built-ins designed sixty years ago for master skeleton keys. These were dual-tumbler dead bolts, two to each door.

They were Elron, Swiss locks. Pickable, but time-consuming.

If Sydney Chong's various collections were as valuable as Francine had said, and they were lying around in open rooms and moldy crates, what could be so much more valuable behind so many sturdy locks?

He padded back to the w.c., flushed loudly, and went down to the second floor.

"Ah, there you are, Frederick." It was Chong, approaching him with an open, felt-lined case. "I've read your book on the Chu Fan Mongol tribesmen. I'd love to have your opinion on this piece."

Carter was thankful his hand was steady as he lifted the fragile piece of earthenware from its case. Carefully, he examined it.

"I regret, Mr. . . . . Sydney," he said at last with a profound shake of his head, "I hate to tell you this, but it's a fake. A clever one, mind you, but a fake nevertheless. You see the finger work here, on the underside of the bowl, and the contour of the lip ridge? I'm afraid this piece was made on a wheel rather than between the knees of the artisan. Worth something, yes, but not the value of a true tenth-century artifact. I would say a clever fifteenth-century reproduction."

"Oh," Chong shrugged, his face doing a marvelous imitation of falling apart. "If only I could afford to have an expert on my staff such as you, I wouldn't make such a fool of myself acquiring fakes. Shall we dine?"

Over Chong's shoulder, Carter saw Francine's shoulders sag with relief.

Lunch was delicious, and through it all, Chong constantly

chatted up Francine. May Won served them, and each time she came near Carter her face lit up in a smile. Twice her breasts brushed his shoulder as she took an empty plate and replaced it with a full one.

By the end of the meal, Carter felt as if they were choosing up sides.

Then the meal was finished and Chong was walking them back to the car.

"You will start tomorrow?"

"Definitely," Carter replied. "With any luck, we should have everything done in two weeks' time."

Chong nodded. "There is no electricity above the first floor except for my office. I will have Johnny Po run some cables into the front wing so you will have light."

"That would be helpful," Francine said.

"Not at all," Chong said graciously. "I can't tell you how proud I am that the institutions you represent are interested in showing my collections. I will see you in a few days' time. I am afraid I must be out of the country for a few days. I have instructed Johnny Po to help you with everything. Good day."

They were driven back to the hotel, and split in front of their rooms.

"Join you for a drink in a minute," Francine said. "I want to crawl into something a little cooler . . . shorts or something."

"Right."

Carter went into his own room and made a beeline to the closet. The closet door and his bag showed smudges. But the hair from his head was still beneath the rivet on the bottom of the bag.

They had searched, but they hadn't found a thing.

By the time he had manufactured Francine's gin and his

own scotch, she rapped on the door.

"Thanks," she said, moving to a chair by the open window. She had changed into a white outfit composed of extremely brief shorts and a halter top. "God, if it's this bloody hot when it rains all the time, what's the dry season like?"

"Unbearable," Carter replied, opening his shirt and taking the chair beside her. "Talk to me."

"He wants to lay me."

Carter grinned. "That was pretty obvious from the moment he took in your chest."

"While you were in the loo, he *suggested* we have dinner in Rangoon some evening."

"And he hinted that it should be just the two of you."

"You're a mind reader," she chuckled. "He's not a very subtle bloke, I'll say that for him. He hinted around, trying to find out if we were sleeping with each other."

"And?"

She hesitated, glancing at him under lowered lids with an enigmatic smile on her face. "I told him we had a purely professional relationship. He said he would send the car for me the day he gets back."

"Good. That could be the night I take a look at the ocean side of the mansion." He went on to tell her about the locked doors he had discovered. "Also, I can't be sure, but I think I saw something on the roof near the rear turret that could have been the counterweight for a crane."

"It's for sure you won't be able to do much investigating inside while we're cataloguing the collection," she replied. "It looks like old baldy Po will be our watchdog all the time we're in the place. God, he gives me the creeps."

Carter chuckled. "I think he's meant to give both of us the creeps. I have to make a call. Be right back."

The Killmaster went downstairs to the lobby. The bar

and lounge were filled with laborers and fishermen. They gave him curious glances, but returned to their drinks and food when he exited to the street.

The shops were all small, specialized to cater to the population of the village. Carter passed each of them, making a mental note. During their walk the previous day, he had spotted the small office of the doctor who had treated him for the head bashing.

A young woman in starchy white looked up from some charts. Carter pointed to his head and explained that he would like an examination, saying his head had been hurting terribly that day.

"I am afraid the doctor will be a few minutes. Please take a seat."

Carter staggered. "I wonder if I could lie down in one of the examining rooms . . . very dizzy . . ."

"Of course."

He followed her down a long hall in the clinic, checking the rooms as he went. Two of them had telephones. The moment she left, he darted from the room he was in to one two doors away. It appeared to be some kind of a lab and file area. There were three buttons on the phone, with three different numbers.

He used the first number to dial the number on the third button. When the nurse/receptionist answered, he put a squeak in his voice and held his nose. "Ah, yes, Long Wee Clinic and Laboratory calling from Rangoon. Please hold for an emergency in your area."

Without waiting for a reply, he hit the hold button and then the button for the second line. Quickly, he direct-dialed the number in Rangoon. A man's voice answered instantly.

"N3, Code Blue, tape please," Carter growled.

There was a click on the line. "Go ahead, N3."

"We are in as of tomorrow. Subject taking flight, perhaps

three days. Could be new area of contact. That's it."

Another click, and the voice came back on the line. "You have local contact. Kuang Bakery has just hired a new apprentice, Kim. He's ours."

Carter killed the connection and raced back to the examination room.

Climbing onto the table, he lay back and sighed. He was glad they had gotten someone in. He was pretty sure that whoever Kim was, he would come in very handy, very soon.

ELEVEN

They spent the first day unloading the crates. Several times, in various ways, Carter tested Johnny Po. Once he wandered directly into the outer wing. The bald man appeared within seconds.

"Place is a maze, isn't it?" Carter said with a laugh. "Good thing you came along. I might have been lost for days."

The man obviously wasn't amused, but he seemed to accept the fact that Carter had simply taken a wrong turn. He didn't move until the Killmaster made a right one and returned to the other wing.

At noon they tried to send Po into the village for larger marking pencils. He was gone, evidently into Chong's office, and reappeared with the pencils in thirty seconds.

Lunch was the same, served by May Won, with Johnny Po not too far away.

It was obvious to both Carter and Francine that he would be their keeper, watchdog, and warden every moment they were in the house.

111

Carter tried to engage May Won in conversation, but learned nothing more than the fact that her English was excellent.

That afternoon, Carter paid a visit to the Kuang Bakery. The only occupants were an old man and old woman. Carter dawdled, taking several minutes to make his choice. In that time, he managed to check out the rear—the oven area—of the shop. There was no one there.

He purchased some rice cakes, then left the shop. Just as he stepped into the street, a youth riding a bicycle with huge baskets fore and aft rode up. He was moving quickly, with the build of a jockey in his work clothes.

One quick look of recognition passed between them, and Carter moved on down the street to the hotel.

The second day was much like the first. On the morning of the third day, Carter told Francine to go on without him.

"Plead my wound to Baldy."

From the window of his room, Carter could see that Johnny Po didn't like the idea of them splitting up, but there wasn't a hell of a lot he could do about it.

The Killmaster idled away the morning, "recuperating" by noon. The hotel proprietor, Sim Dok, and his sister looked as though one of them would follow when he left, but after winding through the village for twenty minutes, there was no one behind him, and he headed for the ocean.

At the commercial fishermen's pier, he found an old, rickety boathouse that also sold supplies. The choice was meager, but Carter managed to buy two stout rods, a couple of reels, and a good-sized tackle box.

A few questions also gave him the proper bait for sea bass and *oofong*, a large type of whitefish in the area.

"You want rent boat?" the old man asked.

"Perhaps another day."

"Off cliffs no catch bass or *oofong*."

Carter walked the cliffs until he sighted the wreck of the old gunboat. Just as they had been the time before, the boys were scampering over the wreck, tending the lines they had attached to the superstructure.

Carter climbed around the hut. After several minutes, he reached the top, then found a path down to the small shallow beach. He was almost to the bottom when the boy shouted, waved with both hands, and dived into the sea. By the time Carter reached the beach, the boy was walking out of the ocean.

"Hello."

"Hello to you," Carter said, noting the way the boy's eyes danced over the gear.

"Where is pretty lady?"

"I'm afraid she had to work today. I'm playing hooky."

"Hooky? What is hooky?"

Carter grinned. "Hooky is fishing. I thought you and I might go for some bass or *oolong*."

The boy's face fell. "Oh, very hard to catch bass or *oolong* this close to shore, even when you are able to cast out." He pointed at the reels.

"I thought perhaps you might know where we could rent a boat."

His face lit up. "Oh, yes, I know . . . but very dear."

Carter handed him a wad of kyats. "Why don't you rent the boat and meet me there, on that point?"

The boy was gone, over the cliffs, running like a deer. He was headed back toward the boat dock where Carter had just purchased the fishing gear. He was sure the old man would wonder where the lad got the money for a boat rental, but he was equally sure that the old man was greedy enough not to look a gift horse in the mouth.

• • •

The boy was good. He could spot the shift in tides that sent the black and gray bodies toward the surface and food. He could also handle the boat, the rod, and the reel like a pro.

By midafternoon, there were five good-sized bass in a bucket in the well of the boat. The boy had caught them all.

They had also sailed south until they were directly off the point, about five hundred yards from Chong's clifftop mansion.

Carter continued to cast and reel in, but he paid very little attention to the fishing. He was laying out in his mind how the cliff could be scaled, and the best approaches to the place once he reached the top.

Also, from this vantage point, even at this distance, he was fairly certain that what he had seen earlier near the southern rear turret was indeed a crane. There was no beach at the foot of the sheer cliff, but also no outcroppings from the cliff itself that would hinder the loading process.

Carter remembered the five boats in Chong's private marina, and how well they were maintained. They could be loaded right there by crane. From there they could sail out to center bay and meet any larger ship leaving Rangoon and heading out to sea. Chances were the ship could be off-loaded the same way whenever the arms were sold.

The boy—Carter had found out by this time that his name was Zenguang and had started calling him Zeke—got another catch.

Carter netted the bass, a big one, into the boat. "One day you'll be the best fisherman on the Burmese coast."

The boy's face flushed. "No. My sister says soon she will send me to school in Rangoon, maybe Singapore or Bangkok, and I will one day be lawyer or doctor and make her proud."

"I have met your sister," Carter said. "There, at Sydney Chong's."

Again a cloud descended over his face at the mention of Chong's name. "I know. My sister told me you work for Mr. Chong."

"No," Carter replied, "we don't work for him." He went on to explain just what he and Francine were doing in the mansion. Carter wasn't surprised that the boy warmed even more to him when he learned that Carter and the pretty lady weren't in league with Chong. "Zeke . . ."

"Yes?"

"You don't like Sydney Chong."

He shrugged. "He is no different than other rich men."

"But your sister works for him."

"No!" He paused, his hands clenched into fists in his lap. "Mr. Chong owns my sister."

Just from his tone, Carter knew he wasn't going to get anything more than that out of the boy. He changed the subject.

"Caught enough?"

"Oh, yes," he said, beaming, "we will feast tonight, my grandfather and I."

Carter started the little outboard. He guided the boat inland as they moved north. About halfway between Chong's mansion and the wreck of the gunboat, he spotted a sandy stretch. Beyond it, almost hidden by the rocks, was a narrow opening that appeared to cut right through the face of the cliff and lead to the inland road.

"That looks to be a fine beach," he commented. "How about a swim before we go in?"

"No, no," Zeke said, a sudden quiver in his voice, "very dangerous."

"Dangerous? It looks to be the best beach around here."

"Mr. Chong's. No fishing, no swimming there. Very private."

"Oh, come on, Zeke, don't tell me you've never gone in there."

Guilt registered on the face and then fear in the eyes. When the denial came, it was too adamant.

Carter shrugged and turned the boat north again. At the wreck, he turned in and beached it.

"Will you return the boat?"

"You do not want any of the fish we catch?"

"Tell you what," Carter said. "You take one of the bass up to the hotel and tell them I want it fixed for the pretty lady's and my dinner tonight. Will you do that?"

He nodded and started gathering the gear.

"No, Zeke, all that is yours."

The boy looked up, his eyes wide. "Mine?"

"Yeah," Carter said, grinning. "But I'd appreciate it if you'd let me use it with you now and then."

"Anytime you want!" Zeke exclaimed happily, and started the small engine, guiding it expertly back out to sea.

Carter set off over the cliffs back toward the village. He stopped across the street from the bakery shop, and studied it in the reflection of a tea shop window.

The old man and woman were in the rear. The young man, Kim, was sweeping out the front. Carter entered the tea shop and sat at a table. A young girl served him. When she went back behind the counter, Carter took out his notepad and a pen, and wrote: *I need underwater night light, a diving belt with weights, flippers, and a mask. If you can have them in the garbage bin behind the hotel by midnight tonight, tell me.*

He folded the note into a ten-kyat bill, and stood.

"May I have more hot water for the tea, please? I'll be right back."

The girl nodded, and Carter crossed the street. Kim rushed behind the counter. Carter handed him the bill.

"Three chocolate rice cakes, fresh and hot. Bring them across the street to me."

"Yes, sir. Oh, yes, sir."

Carter returned to the tea shop. Five minutes later, Kim came running across the street with the rice cakes. He gave them to the girl, who turned and carried them to Carter.

Over the girl's shoulder, Carter saw the young man nod, turn, and leave the shop.

Carter finished his cakes and tea, paid, and left the shop.

Francine was in his room, sipping gin, when he returned.

"You recovered," she said.

"About noon. Went fishing with the boy from the hut . . . May Won's brother."

"Bully for you."

"Dress for dinner. I'm taking you to the best restaurant in town."

"There's only one," she chuckled.

"I know—that's where we're going. And then we're making great preparations for bed, and then we're going to bed . . ."

Her eyes grew wide, "We are?"

"And then, my proper little intellectual, we're going trolling."

Promptly at nine, Carter crossed the hall and rapped on Francine's door. She opened it, and Carter's libido did a little jig. She was dressed in a tailored black silk slack-and-blouse outfit. No skin was showing, not an inch, but she was pure sex from her green eyes to her bright red toenails peeking from her flat-heeled sandals.

"You look sensational," he said.

"I know," she giggled. "I'll be the belle of Kamwaddy."

"No doubt about it."

He took her arm and they descended to the bar as if they were entering the dining room of the Ritz.

Francine turned all eyes. Carter guided her to a corner table, and the eyes followed. He ordered drinks from a tight-lipped Sim Li, and the eyes watched them drinking.

"We're certainly the center of attention," Francine said dryly.

"You are," he said, smiling. "How was your day?"

"Just like yesterday and the day before. Thank God that girl, May Won, was up there. I don't think I'd like to be in that place alone with Baldy. And your day?"

"We're about to dine on it," Carter said.

To his surprise, the bass was perfectly prepared and delicious, redolent with ginger and scallions. Throughout the drinks, the meal, and the dessert, he played the amorous lover. He held Francine's hands, lit her cigarettes, and caressed her cheek. He looked at her adoringly and fawned over every caustic comment she made, as if she had just spoken of eternal love or imparted the wisdom of the ages.

"Would you mind telling me what the hell is going on?" she finally muttered under her breath.

"Why, Fran, darling, you mean at your age you don't recognize a man wooing you?"

"Merde," she hissed.

"True, but hopefully to the rest of the world, it looks like woo."

At ten they ascended the stairs, hand in hand.

"What now? Or do I dare ask," she murmured as they reached the door to her room.

"You put a nightgown and robe on over a pair of jeans and a dark sweatshirt. Then you go down to the w.c. and do your evening toilette. Then you return to my room and we go to bed."

"Together?"

"That's the general idea."

"Lovely. I don't have a nightgown. I sleep in the nude."

"Do you have a robe?" he asked through clenched teeth.

"Yes."

"Then use that."

"Lovely." She disappeared behind her door.

Carter peeled off to his own room. He stripped and got into bed. He heard her pad down the hall, and a few minutes later she slipped into his room. He heard her removing her clothes.

"Were they out there?" he asked.

"God, yes, as usual. There is always one of them checking on us. Damn!"

"What's the matter?"

"I can't see."

"Well, turn on the light," he chuckled.

She did.

Carter blinked. She was standing, barefoot, in bra and panties, folding her jeans over the back of a straight-backed chair. She was big, nowhere an ounce of fat, tall, taut, beautifully proportioned.

She glanced over her shoulder. "Mind telling me what this is all about?" she whispered.

"Around three, we're going out. In the meantime, we sleep."

"Okay."

She killed the light. Carter rolled toward the wall and willed his body to relax, sleep. When, after ten minutes, she hadn't come to bed, he sat up.

"Fran . . ."

"Yes?"

"Where are you?"

"Over here."

"Over where?"

"In the easy chair."

He turned on the bedside light. She was curled up in the easy chair under her robe.

"What the hell are you doing over there?"

"Sleeping. Or trying to."

"Why don't you get into bed?" he asked.

"You didn't ask me. Besides, if I'm going to be seduced, I'd rather it be done by style rather than command."

"Oh, Christ," Carter sighed exasperatedly. "If you're going to be a prig, take the bed."

She laughed. "Pronounce that again."

"*Prig,*" he said pointedly. "Go to bed. I'll take the chair."

"Very gallant. Forget it."

"I insist."

"Forget it. You're the host, I'm the guest. The host gets the bed. I'm well brought up. Those are the rules of the game."

Carter rolled from the bed and crossed to the chair. "Take the bed then. I'll take the chair."

"No."

"Stubborn."

"Yes," she said. "I don't know if I can sleep with you platonically."

Carter couldn't help a roar of laughter. He flipped the robe from her. "C'mon."

She stood up. No bra, no panties. Just body. "All right."

She slipped her arm through his and—nakedly but quite formally—they proceeded to the bed.

Carter snapped off the light and crawled in. Francine slithered in behind him.

"Good night," she said.

"Half night," he replied. "We arise at three, remember?"

"Three it is."

She turned onto her right side and he onto his left. Their buttocks touched, warmly.

He made no move.

Neither did she.

TWELVE

When his watch buzzed, Carter awakened at once. Beside him he could feel Francine stirring.

"Time?"

"Yeah," he whispered. "Get dressed, no lights. Let's go."

He had already worked on the rear window of his hotel room so that it would open without a sound. They crawled through, and moved along a ledge to a corner drainpipe. He was glad to see that Francine moved deftly, without fear.

On the ground, he signaled her to wait, and belly-crawled to the garbage bin.

Kim had done his job well. The gear was in a black, watertight bag. Carter retrieved it and crawled back to where Francine waited.

"This way. We'll go inland up those hills and bypass the main part of the village."

For twenty minutes they climbed, then moved along the ridge until the main part of Kamwaddy was behind them. Here, Carter fell on his belly and motioned her down beside him.

They lay on a rock ledge, squinting down at the sprinkling

of huts that lined the road north of the village proper. The
sky was overcast and there was a thick white mist coming
in off the sea.

"Perfect," he murmured.

"Just what are we up to?" Francine whispered at his elbow.

"Two things. This afternoon, I think I spotted a back way
up to the house. I want to check it out. Also, there's a little
cove with a beach that the boy was afraid to go into. I want
to take a look at that. Let's go!"

They went off the ledge and down the slope, skirting the
huts, and eventually coming to the sea.

"Here's where we go in. Strip, and put your clothes and
shoes in the bag."

They both quickly undressed down to the shorts they had
worn under their clothes. With the clothes stowed in the
bag, they slipped into the water. Carefully, they made their
way past the jagged rocks and swam south.

It was about a quarter of a mile before they were just out
from the boathouse.

"Can you float out here for about five minutes?" he asked.

"No problem."

He draped the bag's strap around Francine's neck and
took off.

The mist was heavier there, obscuring most of the headland. He swam around the angled breakwater of the tiny
harbor, with its tin sheds and the gently tossing masts of a
few boats.

He moved silently among the boats. It was difficult to
see more than a few yards ahead, but in the second line he
found what he wanted: a shallow-bottomed, skiff-style rowboat.

It would be fast and quiet.

From the pocket in his shorts he took a pick, and seconds

later the padlock snapped open. He wound the chain around the mooring hook so it wouldn't rattle, and unfastened the painter.

Soundlessly, he pushed the boat, at the stern, back out around the breakwater and toward the open bay where Francine waited.

"No, not yet," he whispered as she threw the bag into the boat and started to get in behind it. "Let's get another fifty or so yards out."

She joined him, and together they covered the distance. Then he rolled into the boat and gave her a hand. He unlocked the oars, and for the next fifteen minutes he rowed south, using the distant lights of Chong's mansion as a beacon.

He stopped, letting the boat drift, when they were directly off the point.

"I'm going in here," he said. "I want you to row steadily in circles, but make sure you don't let the tide take you in. Got that?"

"Got it."

As Carter spoke, he slipped into the water. "If anything should happen in there, I'll raise enough hell so you can hear it."

"Then what do I do? Row this bloody thing across the bay to Rangoon?"

He chuckled. "No, you head back toward Kamwaddy. Beach this thing anywhere, and go directly to the bakery shop. You know it?" She nodded. "Rap on the back door. The boy's name is Kim. He's ours, and he'll get you out."

She reached out and tentatively touched his hand where it gripped the rail. "Do me a favor?" she whispered. "Don't let anything happen."

"I don't plan on it," he told her, and rolled backward off the bow into the water.

He struck off into the mist at a steady crawl. Closer to shore the tide tried to take him, but he managed to work with it and get past the deadly rocks. He landed only a few feet from the spot he had seen from the boat while fishing that afternoon.

Carefully, he moved along the rocks until he was directly below the house. Then he slipped back into the water and, as he dived, flipped on his light.

It didn't take long to find what he had already guessed was there.

Mooring rings, over twenty of them driven strategically into the rocks. The boats could pull right up to the cliff, a diver could go down and anchor them, and they could be leisurely loaded no matter how strong the ocean was running.

He had seen enough. Flipping off the light, he swam back to the spot where he had entered, and climbed out. He rested a minute, then got out of his gear. When it was stacked, high and dry, he began the climb upward.

It didn't take long to find a worn set of steps. They were obviously man-made, hacked right out of the stone.

Carter checked the stiletto in his belt, and started up. The mist had made the steps slick, but in his bare feet he made good time. Halfway up, the path changed direction and got steeper.

Above him, he could vaguely see the nearest tower of the mansion partially obscured by the mist that rolled against the headland, draping trees and hills in a pulsating blanket.

And then the steps ended, right up against the foundation. Sheer stone and brickwork rose above him for a good fifty feet.

Half by sight and half by feel, he found a worn path along the foundation to a steel gate. It was locked, but through the judas-hole he could see a tiny courtyard area and another door.

Grimly, he nodded to himself. He had found the way in.

He retraced his steps, and was almost at the corner above the steps when he heard the sound, a shoe against stone.

He melted into the shadows and stood motionless.

A short, chunky man stepped around the corner and stopped. A cigarette hung from his lips, and he had a shotgun cradled in his arm.

So, Carter thought, *it wasn't just Johnny Po who watchdogged the place.*

Then the man took a deep drag on his cigarette. The glow illuminated his face, and Carter recognized him. He was one of the three who had waylaid him and Francine and taken their passports and visas.

Carter tensed his right arm. If the man moved his way, Hugo—the Killmaster's stiletto—would be in his throat before he took two steps.

As Carter watched, the cigarette glowed again. Then it flew outward and disappeared over the cliff. The man stretched, yawned, and moved away, around the corner and out of sight.

Carter sighed with relief and dropped into a crouch to wait for the man's footsteps to die away. When they did, he moved to the steps and started down.

He had more than enough now. The place was well guarded, and it was a cinch that Sydney Chong was guarding a lot more than art and antiquities. There was definitely a means of transporting goods by sea. It was a pretty sure bet that those goods weren't just pottery, or they could be moved a lot more easily out the front door.

Now there was only one thing more to check.

At the bottom of the steps, Carter donned his gear and slid into the water. As soon as he was clear of the rocks, he headed north toward the little cove that had so frightened Zeke.

At the sandy beach, he climbed out and inspected the opening through the cliff. It was about ten feet wide and the bottom was fairly smooth rock. It was pitch dark when he moved under the overhang, so he snapped on the light.

Twenty yards farther on, he could see that it was a cave with two openings: one to the sea, and the other to a lane that led up through the cliffs right to the road that went to the house.

This, Carter thought, probably served as their escape hatch. They could get away through here to a boat if the mansion was besieged. Also, if a daylight pickup or delivery was needed, there was room for a small truck or a three-wheeler to get through the cave and on-load or off-load from a boat.

No wonder Sydney Chong had made the little cove off limits to the villagers.

He killed the light until he was back in the water and diving. Now he would clarify his second hunch. The undersea shelf fell of drastically just a few feet from the beach. He rolled over and went down, turning the light on and using only his flippers.

About thirty yards in front of him—and at a deeper depth—he saw something rising up off the ocean floor. It rolled grotesquely, gyrating slowly with the movement of the water.

It was some sort of vehicle.

Carter swam toward it until he could see part of a mutilated hand and forearm protruding from the driver's seat. Then he saw the staring white smile of a dead face, lidded eyes, and swollen mouth.

He went up for a gasp of air and dived again. What was left of a man was a swollen marionette of clothing, bones, and fish food. The water ballooned inside a khaki shirt, and the legs were bent, flopping oddly under the tightly fastened seat belt.

Carter made sure the vehicle was a Land-Rover, and then memorized the license plate. The rear seat and passenger seat had been removed, as had one of the front wheels.

He knew where the passenger seat was. The rear seat and the wheel had probably been sold. He couldn't really blame Zeke. It was a matter of survival. The man was dead. Nothing could help him now. But parts of the Rover could be used or sold.

The Killmaster snapped off the light and surfaced, gulping for air. He floated, coughing and spitting, for a few moments, then began to swim out toward the boat.

Francine helped him into the boat, and as he stripped the gear from his body, he knew his face must be talking.

"You found something," she said.

"Yeah. Remember I told you we sent a man in before, name of Charlie Verrain?"

She nodded.

"Well, I just found him. Or what's left of him."

Her head swiveled toward the cove. "Down there?"

"Yeah," Carter growled, dipping the oars into the water, "down there."

Back in the room, they dried themselves in the dark and Carter poured two stiff drinks. Outside, false dawn was just starting to break.

He stood by the window, smoking. He had wrapped a towel around his waist.

Francine was sitting in the easy chair with her knees pulled up under her, her hands clasping her knees and her chin resting on them. She was staring at Carter pensively.

"What happens now?" she asked softly.

"We hope Chong gets back soon and he still has the hots for you." Out of the corner of his eye he saw her shiver. "Come here."

She was more than willing. She crossed to join him, slipping under his arm and moving close, her head on his chest, his arm around her shoulder.

"You said this could get messy."

He nodded. "And it has. If Chong shows up, I want you to agree to join him in Rangoon for dinner."

"In other words, you want to get me out of the way."

"Something like that," he replied, crushing out his cigarette and picking up his drink. "I'll arrange, through Kim, to have you watched with Chong in Rangoon. They'll find a way for you to slip away and hide you."

"And while I'm slipping away and hiding . . . ?"

"I take another rowboat ride." He looked down at her and smiled. "Only this time I won't need to have anyone rowing in circles waiting for me."

"Oh?"

"I'll be going out the front door instead of back into the ocean."

She slipped her arm around his waist. "God, it must be nice to think of yourself as superman."

"It's what I'm here for. Why don't you get some sleep?"

"Sleep? Are you bloody nuts?" she gasped. "I'm as tight as a piano wire. Who can sleep while you're standing here figuring out a way to get yourself killed!"

"Ah, ye of little faith. I'm an expert, remember?"

"Yeah, I know," she sighed. "Besides, we'd only have to get up in an hour or so."

"True."

They stared at the mounting light for another few seconds, and then she tilted her head up and kissed him. Carter responded at once, pulling her to him tightly as an electric shock arced between them.

Her body pressed against his. Her lips parted to let his tongue probe her mouth. His hand moved beneath her robe and found her naked thigh.

"I don't think I could sleep either," he said huskily, his lips only a fraction from hers, "but I don't rule out bed."

"Neither do I," she replied, shrugging her shoulders out of the robe. As it fell to the floor, she twisted the towel from his hips and dropped it to join her robe.

He lifted her across the few feet to the bed and lay her across it. She tugged him down beside her and molded her body to his.

"You planned this all along, didn't you?" she asked, her perfect teeth gleaming in a smile.

"I never plan . . . this."

His hand cupped her full breast as his other hand entwined in her hair. One finger lightly stroked the tip of her breast, feeling it grow hard. His mouth explored her whole body now, traveling over the pulse in her throat, her shoulder, her breast.

Francine moaned, a low, animal sound deep in her throat.

Carter's lips continued their erotic journey. His tongue lightly flicked the tips of her nipples and his teeth gently bit the heaving swell of her breast. Then his lips moved to her waist and stomach. Her hips arched against him, then instinctively began to move slowly, rhythmically.

Suddenly she cried out, tugging him up over her body. "No, don't tease . . . no more . . ."

He was above her now, looking down at the mask of passion that was her face. She had become a writhing volcano, and he let her do it all.

Her hands found him. She caressed and then pulled him

to her. She groaned loudly as their bodies met, and Carter felt a quiver roll like the ocean's tide over her flesh.

She widened her legs, and her hips rose to meet his penetration, which was sudden and forceful. He went all the way to her deepest recesses, and then he began working in and out, slowly at first, as she moaned and bit his shoulder in passion. She moved, too, undulating her surging body upward, in a circular motion, always straining to recapture him every time he felt as if he would leave her.

He placed his hands under her buttocks, to give her extra impetus every time her hips rose. She whimpered, convulsed, and her motions became more frantic. She cried out again. Her quivering intensified. Sweat ran off both their bodies, and still she came forward, her movements demanding, insisting, almost uncontrolled.

She gasped between groans now, and the gasps synchronized with his heavy breathing and matched his rhythm. He allowed himself full freedom, no longer trying in any way to withhold from her the ultimate result of her urgings to his body.

As the two of them nearly rose off the bed, arched like a bow on the now warm and damp sheets, he exploded, sending himself violently into her. In one giant simultaneous orgasm, Francine cried out one last time, her entire body tensed like steel, and then they both collapsed.

THIRTEEN

Early the next morning, Carter went to the bakery. He bought rice cakes and passed a detailed note to the boy. Chong was due back that day, and Carter guessed that he would ask Francine to accompany him to Rangoon that evening.

In the note he gave Kim, he gave full instructions on picking up Francine as soon as she could shake Chong. He also included what he knew thus far, and told them he was planning on going in.

He wasn't surprised when he got a note himself in return with his change. He slipped it into his pocket and returned to the hotel.

Johnny Po was waiting with the limo. Francine was just emerging from the front door. Carter held up the small package.

"Rice cakes for lunch."

A new Mercedes was in the drive when they arrived.

"We have visitors today?" Carter asked.

"Mr. Chong," Johnny Po replied.

They worked at the collection for a half hour, and then Carter slipped off to the w.c. and opened the note.

*Manila picked up on one Raul Donato . . . believe him
to be contact, most likely Oheda's replacement . . . trailed
subject to Jakarta, where he managed to disappear . . .
sorry. No sign of Sydney Chong after flying out of Rangoon
on private jet . . . research assumes a deal has been made.*

Jolly, Carter thought, just jolly, as he tore up the note
and flushed it away.

It was nearly noon when May Won appeared to tell them
that Mr. Chong awaited them in the courtyard for lunch.

As they were going down the stairs, the girl clutched
Carter's sleeve, holding him back. When Francine moved
on ahead, the girl spoke.

"Thank you for being a friend to my brother. He likes
you very much. He says you are a good man. I am in your
debt."

Before Carter could reply, she had tripped on ahead.

Behind the first floor of the house was a black flagstone
terrace that gave way to a wide sweep of lawn fanning out
to the sheer cliff above the ocean on one side and a high
stone wall on the other.

Sydney Chong was on the terrace, sitting on a stool by
a low wall. Just as Carter hit the door, he saw Chong raise
a rifle and fire. Carter looked to his left and saw a clay
skeet shatter in the air. Chong quickly discarded the rifle
and came up with another gun from between his legs.

Carter stepped out onto the patio and joined Francine.
She was gritting her teeth.

Johnny Po, with a sawed-off shotgun slung behind one
shoulder, was pulling the lever of a mechanism set up on
one side of the green. A white clay disk shot out of it and
arced high in the air. Chong, standing where the terrace
edged the lawn, followed the target with a long-barreled
Beretta skeet shotgun, and squeezed the trigger. The clay
disk shattered into a thousand pieces.

"Is this for our benefit?" Francine hissed.

"Who knows?" Carter replied, guiding her forward with a hand on her arm.

Chong handed the Beretta to Johnny Po when he saw them. "Ah, here we are. You're looking radiant today, Francine."

"Thank you," she said, managing a smile.

Chong kissed her hand and turned to Carter. "And, Frederick, how is the work going?"

"Very well," Carter replied, grasping the man's hand and forcing himself not to wince when the knuckles were worked together in Chong's grasp.

A pair of disks were released. Johnny Po fired with the rifle. One disk exploded, and in a millisecond, he had unslung the sawed-off from his back and nailed the second.

Chong turned to Carter and raised an inquiring eyebrow. "What do you think?"

Carter shrugged. "I rather imagine that was quite good. Frankly, I know very little about guns."

"Ah, too bad," Chong replied. "I thought you might like to try."

"No, thank you," Carter said. "I'm afraid I would just waste the ammunition."

"I'd like to try," Francine announced.

All three of the men turned at once to stare at her. Finally, Chong spoke. "Of course, Francine. Please do."

She expertly loaded the Beretta, and then picked up the shotgun and levered a fresh cartridge into the chamber. She glanced over at Johnny Po.

"Load . . . two."

The man shrugged, then loaded the launcher. Francine splayed her feet, took a stance, and raised the rifle.

"Pull!" One disk arced high in the air. At a second command, the second followed.

Taking her time, she carefully followed the first disk with the rifle. She got the trajectory, then led it a bit. As the target reached the top of its arc, just before it headed down, she gently squeezed the trigger.

Just as the first disk exploded, she flipped the rifle to an astounded Johnny Po. In the same movement, she rolled the shotgun off her shoulder. The move was almost a blur as she brought it to her shoulder and fired. It didn't look as though she was hurrying, though she had only a split second left when she fired.

The second disk shattered just before it disappeared over the edge of the cliff.

Calmly, she turned and tossed the Beretta to Johnny Po.

"My husband taught me. Shall we have lunch, gentlemen?"

The invitation was extended to Carter as well as Francine, but the Killmaster could see that Chong wasn't pushing it too hard. He begged off, but urged Francine to go ahead.

They left right after lunch, in the Mercedes, with Chong driving. Johnny Po was left with Carter.

It wasn't too long after lunch when Carter saw the men arriving. The cars were parked in the trees at the bottom of the drive near the wall, and the men walked up toward the house and disappeared around the corner.

He called down and requested tea from May Won. When she brought it, he asked casually about the men.

"Sailors" was her only reply.

From the side window, he spotted the men working on the boats in the marina. They looked as if they were getting ready for the sea.

Tonight, he thought, *is the night!*

Later in the afternoon, Carter went downstairs. As usual,

the bald man appeared immediately.

"I've decided I need a little time off, too. If you'll be so kind as to take me back to the hotel, I think I'll get a little fishing in."

At the hotel, Carter changed clothes and composed a message for Rangoon to be sent through Kim. Trying to use any telephone in the village would be far too dangerous.

He had tea at the little shop across from the bakery, but no Kim. He knew he would have to go with his alternate plan, when the little owner of the hotel, Sim Dok, strolled in and, animatedly, sat down at Carter's table.

"Your room good, Mr. Ellison?"

"Five-star," Carter replied dryly.

"That good. I see your lady friend in big car with Mr. Chong. She no visit you tonight?"

The man's mouth was all teeth between thin, widespread lips. Carter imagined putting him against the wall for twenty minutes and then sending him off to a dentist.

"If you'll excuse me, I think I'll do a bit of fishing." Carter stood, but the man's voice stopped him at the door.

"Maybe you like girlfriend tonight? Young girl? Very nice?"

"No, thanks."

At the boat dock, he rented a small outboard and putt-putted his way to the wreck. Zeke was there, alone, with both reels.

"Hello, Fred, how are you?"

"I'm fine, Zeke. Mind if I join you?"

"Oh, no, please do."

Carter moved in beside him on the old wreck's superstructure and took over one of the reels. For about fifteen minutes, they chatted and fished before Carter brought it up.

"Zeke, I've made another friend in the village. I wonder

if you'd mind if he fished with us."

"Oh, no. Who?"

"His name is Kim. He works at the bakery. Would you mind running into the village and telling him to join us after he leaves work tonight?"

"No, I get him."

"And, Zeke . . ."

"Yes?"

"Don't bring him here. Swim out from the rocks beyond your hut and go to the wreck. Enter the superstructure from the seaward side. I'll meet you inside."

For the first time since Carter had met him, the boy looked wary and suspicious. His hands came together in his lap and worked each other. His brow furrowed, and he stared at Carter questioningly.

"I don't understand . . ."

"It's very difficult to explain, Zeke. First of all, I think we both agree that Sydney Chong is a very bad man. Yes?"

The boy averted his eyes. His neck disappeared down into his shoulders, and for a full minute he seemed to ponder this.

"Yes," he whispered finally. "He is an evil man. Long ago, my father worked for Mr. Chong. One day, Johnny Po came to our house. He tells my father that he wants to take May Won away, send her to school. He wants to buy May Won. My father got very angry. He shouted at Johnny Po that he would never let May Won be the . . ."

Tears filled the boy's eyes, and it seemed for a moment that he wouldn't be able to continue. Then he squared his frail shoulders and looked up, directly into Carter's eyes.

"He would never let May Won be the whore of Sydney Chong. Not long after that, my father was lost at sea.

"How do you know all of this, Zeke?"

"Some I remember. My grandfather, he tells me the rest. A little while after our father is gone, Johnny Po comes again. My mother has no choice, now we are very poor."

"And what happened to your mother?"

"She became very sick. She died. My grandfather is very sad. He tells me many things, and then he goes away . . . up here." Zeke pointed to his head. "And he never speaks again. I hate Sydney Chong."

Carter played with the reel for a moment, weighing the situation. "Zeke, I've been sent here to stop Sydney Chong from doing many bad things that you wouldn't understand. I know about the seat that your grandfather sits on . . . the one from the Rover."

The boy's eyes flashed and his face flushed with guilt. "I saw them the night they drove the machine into the water. Johnny Po and the police. I didn't know there was a man in it until I swam down to it. But after I was there . . ." He shrugged.

"I know, Zeke. Would you like to help me?"

"Are you a policeman?"

"In a way," Carter said, nodding. "But I'm not a policeman like the prefect, Sin Chai."

"Will you kill Sydney Chong?"

"Perhaps. It will depend on many things. But after tonight, you and your sister will be free of him."

The boy, almost smiling now, said, "Then I will help you."

Carter reached over and tousled his hair. "And get us some sweet rice cakes while you're there . . . and enough for your grandfather while you're at it."

Carter gave him money, and he was off like a shot. He slipped a cigarette between his lips just as both rods started bending.

God, he thought, *the kid's a great fisherman and he isn't even here!*

It was after dark when Carter pulled around the point and dropped the stone anchor over the side. He knew he had been watched from the cliff for the last hour, but doubted if the watcher would come down and investigate if the bow light was left on and the two rods were played out in the water.

He stripped and, leaving his clothes and shoes in the boat, slipped into the water. He swam out to the edge of the rocks, but dared go no farther lest he be seen. That meant judging the swells and picking his way through the jagged outcroppings in water that ranged from his knees to somewhere over his head.

Reaching the wreck, he pulled on a rope hanging from the stern, and a rope ladder tumbled from the deck into the water.

He chuckled to himself. In America, young boys would have a tree house to play in. In Southeast Asia, it was the wreck of an old gunboat, and they had the advantage of fishing from it.

Carter wasn't too sure the latter wasn't preferable. It built more character.

He clambered up the ladder to the deck at the wreck's stern, keeping low. The cloud cover was heavy and there was a light rain, but he wasn't taking any chances that the party or parties on the cliff had night glasses.

He pulled the ladder back to the deck and moved slowly along the slippery, slanted deck amidships. He could hear the sea gurgling noisily through the hull beneath the deck, and Zeke's explanation came back to him:

"The sea moves through a hole in the stern and out again

through a hole in the bow. But there is no need for worry. The boat will not move. It is held fast by the rocks."

Carter moved through an open hatchway into a central salon. It was dimly illuminated in gray through rusty cracks. He breathed the musty odor of damp wood and rust mingling with the tang of saltwater. Out of the salon, he picked his way along a short passage, ending abruptly against a sliding door.

He knocked, and the door swung wide at once. Zeke stood to the side, and across a small cabin he saw the older boy, Kim, with a Mauser in both hands. The moment he saw Carter, he slid the gun into his belt.

"You're lucky I came. I was against it at first, but the kid was convincing." He spoke English with a British accent.

"Nice to be able to speak to you out front for a change," Carter said. "Kim, is it?"

He nodded. "It's really Kim." He glanced toward Zeke, whose wide eyes were darting between them.

"It's okay," Carter said, patting the boy's shoulder. "He's one of us."

Kim shrugged. "What's up?"

"First," Carter said, "have they got eyes on Chong and the woman?"

Kim nodded. "Since they left Kamwaddy in the Mercedes this afternoon."

Carter checked his watch. "Okay, she's going to split from Chong at the Café of Golden Dreams in about two hours. I want our people ready to pick her up and get her out of there."

"No problem. What else?"

"Johnny Po is moving the stuff out tonight by boats. My guess is they meet a freighter out of Rangoon, either some-time tonight or early morning. Hopefully, I'll disrupt the loading before the boats get away."

"You're going in?" Kim asked.

Carter nodded. "If I miss the boats, do we have the man-power to shadow the freighters?"

Kim bit his lip and shook his head. "Not really. But we could put a two-man boat at the mouth of the bay and follow them out to the freighter. If we get the name, we can mess up the off-loading at the other end."

"That will have to do," Carter said. "Have you got hardware?"

Kim smiled in such a way that it added years to his face, and patted his belt. "Besides this, I've got six M-1 grenades, an Aussie Austen sub with a ton of ammo, and two Spitzer ground-launched rockets."

Carter shook his head. "It sounds like you expected this."

"Not really," he said, and shrugged. "It's my usual travel-ing gear. Where do you want me after I pass on to Rangoon?"

"Midnight sharp by the front gate," Carter said. "But stay under cover, even when you hear the banging start. I mainly want you for backup to cover my ass. But it might not be a bad idea to set up those two Spitzers when you arrive, just in case."

"What if you're getting the worst of it?"

"Then play it by ear and come ahead," Carter said, and turned to the boy. "Zeke, I want you to leave right now. Go up to the house and get your sister. Tell her your grand-father is bad, he might die. She must come with you at once. Do you have anyplace besides the hut or here where the three of you can hide until this is over?"

"I have. There are many caves north of the village."

"Good. Use one of them, and don't come out until you see Kim or me waving a sheet from the roof of the hotel. Okay?"

"Okay." The boy seemed to hesitate.

"What is it?" Carter asked.

"You blow up house to hell?"

Carter nodded. "Something like that."

"Johnny Po will go to his ancestors?"

"There's a fairly good chance of that," Carter said, "yeah."

"But Sydney Chong is in Rangoon. He won't be in house."

"Don't worry about Sydney Chong," Carter said evenly. "He'll be taken care of."

FOURTEEN

Carter returned the boat and walked to the hotel. The bar was nearly empty. Sim Dok was in his usual place at the piano; an old woman Carter had seen a time or two in the kitchen was behind the bar. There were a couple of idlers sucking rice wine at one of the tables.

"Oh, Mr. Ellison, how was the fishing?" Sim Dok asked, breaking into a sort of Chinese rendition of "Feelings" on the ancient piano.

"Lousy," Carter said, and ordered a scotch, neat, from the old woman.

"Too bad. Since your lady friend is not here tonight, perhaps you would like a game of chess? I'm sure you play chess, don't you, Mr. Ellison?"

"Afraid not. And, anyway, I think I'll turn in early tonight."

"Very well," Sim Dok said as Carter mounted the stairs, "Happy dreams."

Carter was inside the room before he smelled the perfume.

"Hello, mister."

Her naked body was stretched across the bed, the legs spread slightly in an erotic pose. The position accentuated

145

the supple smoothness of her deliciously curved flesh. The firm shapes of her small-nippled breasts were upthrust by the strained position.

"Does your brother know where you are, Sim Li?" Carter snapped the lock on the door and started edging toward the closet.

"Of course. He don't mind. You very big man. I like big men. Come to bed with Sim Li, I give you good time all night."

"How much, Sim Li?" He was casually unbuttoning his shirt as he moved.

She spread her legs a little more and cupped her breasts with her hands. "Why you ask that? Sim Li no whore."

She was worth looking at. Her skin was like flowing honey. Her body was small and slim, accentuating the youthful ripeness of breasts, loins, and buttocks. But what made her beauty so exotic was a startling contrast: her dark hair, disheveled now, framed a lovely face that was pure Chinese except for the lean, high-bridged nose.

Carter yanked open the closet door. His bag was gone. Behind him, he heard Sim Li's feet hit the floor. He lunged, hitting her hip-high and sending her sailing against the far wall. She wheeled off the wall and opened her mouth to scream.

The stiletto flashed in Carter's right hand. "Don't," he hissed.

She gave up the scream, probably to throw Carter off, because she moved, fast. She came at him, her left hand extended, palm up and fingers stiff, her right hand pulled back alongside her head, ready to strike.

He spun as he ducked, and the outside edge of his right boot caught her just above the left elbow. Her right hand slashed down through space where he'd been standing, but all it hit was air. Still pivoting, he brought his right hand down and caught her with the hardened edge just below the skull on her pretty neck. She landed on her side and slid to a stop just short of the door.

"Try that again," Carter growled, "and I'll use the blade."

For an answer, she screamed bloody murder and lurched toward the locked door. Carter caught her wrist just in time and spun her away from the door. Like an acrobat, she vaulted the bed and, screaming, came at him again.

Already the Killmaster could hear feet bounding up the stairs. It was obvious that they had this all set up. But why? What had tipped them off?

Carter met her head-on. She caught him with both hands to the neck, and sank her teeth in his forearm before he could use the blade. The stiletto slipped from his hand.

There was pounding on the door.

Carter managed to pull his head to one side as he felt himself go down. Consequently, her knee grazed his cheek instead of catching him full in the face. At the same time, she brought her right hand down in a vicious chop at his neck. Had the blow struck as intended, she would probably have killed him. But his momentum threw her off and he felt the impact high on his shoulder, where it did little damage. He crashed into her and his weight carried her into the wall.

He started to roll to one side but wasn't quite fast enough to escape the pair of smooth brown legs that scissored around his head. He continued to roll, but she rode him like a rodeo cowboy until she was kneeling with her calves locked beneath him and his head squeezed tightly between her thighs, his mouth and nose covered by her flesh. He couldn't breathe as she put all of her strength and the full weight of her body into the grip.

Carter tried to grab her, but his right hand got tangled in the bed sheets and his left arm was pinned beneath him.

Drawing up his knees, he gathered his strength for one mighty heave, when she suddenly relaxed her hold and fell sideways. He rolled clear, but it still took a second to get oriented.

The stiletto had caught between the bed leg and its support, with the rear of the hilt to the floor. When Sim Li had rolled, the blade had gone right through her neck, windpipe to spine.

Carter reached for the hilt just as the door behind him flew open. It was Sim Dok and a uniformed policeman. Sim Dok was just bringing up the revolver in his hands when Carter came up off the floor.

He did everything in one fluid move. With his head, he butted the gun up so the slug shattered the plaster ceiling. Hugo's point went between the fifth and sixth ribs, and ended Sim Dok's life instantly when it hit the heart.

In the same motion, Carter shoved the dead man into the live one. They tumbled into the hall and Carter slammed the door.

Breathing heavily now, he threw open the window and went through. His toes barely touched the ledge as he made his way to the drainpipe and slid to the ground on his insteps.

There was a shout and then a shot from the window. The slug tore into the wall a foot from Carter's head, and he moved down the alley as fast as his feet could carry him.

He was almost to the end of the alley when a car, no lights, suddenly roared out in front of him. There was no way he could stop.

He slammed into the fender and over the hood with the force of a pile driver. He felt the stiletto leave his hand and saw it skitter away in the mud.

Three of them came at him before he could raise himself from the muddy street. Two were in uniform and the third was one of the idlers he had seen in the bar.

Carter came up hard into the first one's gut with his head. As he went over, the Killmaster chopped the back of his neck.

One down, two to go.

Wrong.

The driver of the car, another uniform, was coming up on his left. The other two were flanking him on the right.

The uniform on his left was moving, and moving too fast for Carter to stop him and keep track of the other two at the same time.

He got hold of Carter's hair and yanked his head back. One of the others jabbed two outthrust fingers at Carter's Adam's apple.

The pain was blinding. He grabbed his throat, unable to breathe.

Legs hit his. Suddenly he was down, the mud oozing around him as fists and boots rained blows on every part of his body.

One of the boots caught the side of his head.

That was the one. He rolled back and let the mud take him.

Carter didn't know how long he was out, but it couldn't have been more than a few minutes.

He didn't move to let them know he was awake as he took stock. His head, neck, and his right side hurt like hell. He smelled and tasted blood, and knew it was his own.

There were four of them, a uniform and the idler in the front. He was sandwiched between two uniforms in the rear. The one on his left was doing all the talking, giving directions. Carter concentrated, and finally recognized the voice: Prefect of Police for Kamwaddy, Sin Chai.

He slitted one eye. They were on the main highway, evidently going north because the ocean was on their left.

Suddenly the car lurched to the right onto a rutted road

and started climbing into the hills. One of the tires hit an especially bad jolt, and Carter could not suppress a yelp of pain.

"Ah, Nick Carter, you are awake," Sin Chai said.

That really jarred him awake. How in hell had his cover been blown, right down to his real name?

"Who?" Carter said hoarsely, breathing still difficult.

"No matter the name," Sin Chai said. "You are charged with murder and you will be shot while trying to escape."

"Self-defense."

Sin Chai's throat gurgled with laughter. "There is no such thing in Burma. You can hasten your death and do away with much pain if, before you die, you tell us a few things we need to know."

"I am a professor of—"

The end of a nightstick wielded by the one on the right went about four inches into Carter's gut, ending any conversation for a while.

As the last lights of Kamwaddy faded behind them, they continued into the hills until their headlights picked up yet another, even smaller, side road. Within minutes they were isolated deep in the dark hills. When they stopped and killed the engine and lights, nothing disturbed the silence or the darkness.

Carter now felt genuinely ill. The rear doors opened and he was yanked from the car. The civilian stood to the side, a shotgun cradled in his arm while the two uniforms held Carter. Prefect Sin Chai stood a couple of feet in front of Carter, his legs apart, his hands on his hips.

"Who are your contacts in Rangoon and what information have you passed on to them?"

"I don't have any contacts in Rangoon," Carter said, only able to whisper.

"How much does the woman, Francine Camway, know,

or have you deceived her as well?"

"We were both sent here to catalogue and evaluate—"

Sin Chai clapped his hands hard together before Carter could finish.

He felt a powerful fist pound into his side. He heard his rib break. He bent forward in agony and jerked backward as the broken bone ripped his insides. While he was concerned with the pain in his body, the same fist slammed into the side of his head. Blood spurted from his cheek and he thought his jaw was broken. He held up his hands to guard against a further assault, but the gesture was futile because the man on the other side of him hit him from that direction. His head exploded again. He turned dumbly to face the new antagonist and caught the same fist again full on the nose. His nostrils split open on both sides and more blood poured forth.

He rocked sideways and back again and then slumped forward. The hard edge of a hand smashed into his back exactly against his kidney, and he fell further forward until he was sprawled on the ground. He knew they were killing him, and the last thing he remembered before slipping into unconsciousness was that he was glad he was dying because it would end the pain.

"That's enough," Sin Chai said. "Pull him back and wake him up."

Where they got the water, Carter didn't know or care. It was life-giving. But he was soon not too sure of that.

"Carter . . .

"Ellison, Frederick Ellison. This is all a dreadful mistake."

"You are hopeless," Sin Chai hissed in his face. "It is important, these questions I ask you, but not imperative. Do you want to die slowly like this, you fool?"

They had him propped up against the car. Slowly, Carter

got his awareness back, flaky as it was.

His head rolled around on his neck and he had difficulty holding it erect. Nausea swept over him and he fought the urge to vomit.

He delicately touched his face, then looked at his fingers. They were covered with blood. He reached for his handkerchief and gingerly wiped the blood from around his mouth, but more spilled over his lips from his nose as fast as he wiped it away.

He finally cupped the handkerchief around his nose until the flow was reasonably under control. He wanted to speak, but he remained silent, fearful he might say something that would cause the assault to begin again. He could hear sound, but the night was so quiet and dark, he knew the sound came from far away.

"Well?" Sin Chai said at last.

Carter decided to go for it. In halting, rasping words, he coughed it out, figuring it would do more good than harm.

"I am an agent of the United States government. We know that you killed Charles Verrain. We know that Sydney Chong is dealing in Vietnamese arms. We know that certain persons in the Burmese government are aiding and abetting these crimes. We know—"

"Enough!" Sin Chai said, slapping Carter soundly with a fierce backhand. "Foutau!"

The civilian with the shotgun stepped forward. *"Pe dou."*

It was all Burmese and Greek to Carter. But he got the drift when the shotgun slammed into his back, propelling him forward. As he moved, Carter assessed the damage.

His face was hamburger and his jaw felt unhinged, but he decided it wasn't broken. There was still a lot of blood, and from the pain in his side it was a cinch that he had at least one or more broken or cracked ribs.

But his arms and legs were usable, and that alone might save him.

The shotgun prodded him through a break in the rocks. There was a clearing on the other side. It had a muddy dirt bottom and a wash running through it on the side. The ground was soft.

"*A ti,*" the man said.

Carter stopped in the center of the clearing and turned. The shotgun toter was grinning like a kid with his first toy, and raising the weapon to his shoulder.

It was clear now what they planned to do: shoot him, then bury him.

Carter tensed. He might as well go down trying.

The man was about to fire. Carter was about to roll to the side.

Suddenly, from the rocks to Carter's left, something silvery hissed through the air. The man gave out with a loud, strangled gasp, dropped the shotgun, and brought his hands up to clutch at his neck.

Carter was on him in an instant. The silvery object was Hugo, his own stiletto. Twenty yards to his left, Kim dropped from the rocks into the clearing.

"Sorry, old chap . . . thought I could take him out on the quiet."

Carter stood staring down at the fresh corpse and then at Kim. The reality of what had just happened was sinking in. Below them, beyond the rocks by the car, he could hear the other three shouting and scrambling. They had been alerted.

"Can you move, old man?" Kim asked.

"Yeah," Carter wheezed. "I can't run a foot race, but I can walk."

"Good show. Cut back over those rocks and flank them.

I'll try to get behind them."

The words were scarcely out of his mouth and he was gone, scampering like a gazelle up the rocks to disappear.

Carter forced the pain out of his mind and wrenched the stiletto from the man's neck. He shoved it, still bloody, back into its sheath and made both his hands work.

He found a box of shells in one of the dead man's pockets, and transferred them to his own. A Webley revolver went from the other's belt to his own, and he snatched up the shotgun.

As fast as his aching body would respond, he scrambled into the far breach of the rocks and out of sight.

He barely made it when there was more shouting from the other side. It was scrambled Burmese and Mandarin, but the Killmaster caught enough words to figure out that one of them had crawled up the rocks enough to peer over and see their dead comrade.

Now he was letting the others know that Carter was loose and armed with the dead man's shotgun.

Good enough, Carter thought, still moving, but slowly, so there would be no noise to guide them. They would assume that he had somehow killed the man and would come after them.

That would leave Kim fairly free to roam.

Carter was well away from the clearing now and angling around. He spotted a break and moved in behind it.

All was quiet, nothing but normal night sounds and the soft patter of the rain. He could see the car. The trunk lid was up, and behind it on the ground was his bag and a couple of shovels.

"Bastards," he hissed to himself, and willed his eyes to sever the blackness and the falling rain. He couldn't find them, but he knew they were there, somewhere, fanning out, trying to find him and finish the job the dead one had screwed up.

He waited another full minute for Kim to work his way well behind their first position, and then he moved farther to his right, keeping the high rocks around him as a shield.

He moved down, using the cover of dead trees and rocks and the dark patches of shadows that they made. He stopped several times to study the rocks ahead from new angles.

The last time he stopped, he saw the man.

He was leaning against a tall spruce, a machine pistol at the ready in both hands. Obviously he was covering the other two and making sure he could spot Carter if the Killmaster tried to get back to the car.

Carter became as motionless as the tree shadow in which he crouched. No part of Carter moved again until he was sure the man had not spotted him.

Carefully, he turned his head and scanned the same area as the watcher. Nothing. No movement, no sound.

Carter could try a blast, but even with the spray of the scatter-gun he might only wound the man since such a small part of him was exposed at this angle.

Wounded, the man could turn and spray with the machine pistol in Carter's direction. The odds were in the enemy's favor if that became the case.

The Killmaster snaked away at an angle from the watcher, keeping his eyes riveted on him all the way. The man didn't move. Carter continued to hug the ground until he reached a thick mass of bramble-type growth. Slipping behind it, he lifted off the ground and moved along its cover in a low crouch.

He knew now that Kim was a seasoned pro. He wouldn't fire from whatever position he had taken until Carter or the enemy made the first move. That gave him the big advantage. They thought they were searching for one man. Kim, as long as he held his fire, had the element of surprise.

Where the brush cover ended, there was another break in the rocks. Carter stood up as he moved into it. His rubber-soled shoes made no sound in the soft, muddy ground as he moved in deeper.

There was a slight muffled cough about ten yards in front of him and to the right. He had flanked the watcher.

The shotgun came up in his hands, ready. Carter was about to move, when the man changed his position. With his machine pistol still at the ready, he stepped into the other end of the shadowy passage. He approached without immediately seeing Carter pressed against the wall.

Carter cursed silently. Where the hell was Kim? His finger was across the shotgun's trigger, but he didn't want to make that much noise yet. He still hadn't reached the right position for it.

Then the man saw him. He stopped dead, the machine pistol twisting in his hands.

Carter had no choice.

The shotgun boomed in the Killmaster's hands. The full charge tore into the man's chest. There was a scream of agony, cut off by death as the man was lifted from his feet and thrown back into the rocks.

An automatic rifle began blasting almost directly above Carter's head, slamming slugs into the stone around the spot he had been. Carter's finger had barely pressed the trigger before he retreated back down the passage between the two rock walls.

He cleared the rocks and dived behind a pair of stunted trees. In the distance he could hear the chatter of a sub-machine gun interspersed with the popping of a rifle.

Kim was on to Number Three.

Carter's man was still firing, the slugs slamming into his tree. He brought the shotgun up, working the pump fast. The automatic rifle was pointing between two craggy rocks, spitting slugs at Carter.

The shotgun roared again. Carter knew he had missed, but the rifle disappeared.

Quickly, Carter reloaded, jamming shells into the chamber of the shotgun as fast as his fingers would work. He could hear the rifleman scrambling down the rocks. If he got to the bottom, he would have clear sight lines to Carter's tree and pin him there indefinitely.

Suddenly a rifle bullet slammed into the tree by his head and he dropped to a prone position, searching.

Something stirred in a deep shadow to his left. He fired, pumped, fired again.

This time he didn't miss. One burst caught the man's arm, practically severing it. He dropped the rifle and lurched to his feet, screaming in pain.

Carter came up on one knee, pumped, and blasted him. The man's body seemed to go back into the rocks in separate sections, practically torn in half.

Carter ran to the rocks and cover. It was quiet now.

"Kim!" Carter shouted.

"Ho!" The voice was about a hundred yards away, but the way it echoed, it was impossible to pinpoint it.

"Two down here!" Carter yelled.

"Proper job," Kim replied. "Number Three is a clever bloke . . . still in my area somewhere!"

Carter hoped Kim was right. He started retracing his steps back toward the original clearing where Kim had killed the first one with Hugo.

He'd gone about twenty feet, when the rifle of Number Three sounded off again, kicking up mud around Carter's feet and ricocheting off rocks around his head.

Damn! he thought. Kim had goofed. Number Three had doubled back.

The Killmaster swerved.

It was a bad move. Without realizing it, he charged right into a clearing.

He would just have to get across it.

He forced every ounce he could from his aching body.

So far, so good. He could barely see the ground beneath his feet as he zigged and zagged. His throat and chest were burning.

Then, halfway across, his foot hit a rock that came out of nowhere. He sailed and hit, hard, the shotgun skittering on a few feet beyond him.

He hit on his right side and yelped in pain, but he managed to roll and come up on one knee. Shaking his head, he searched the ground for the weapon.

But he saw a pair of legs first. His eyes traveled up to the gleaming eye of Prefect Sin Chai. The eye was gleaming over the barrel of what looked like an elephant gun.

"You have five seconds to tell your friend, whoever he is, to come forward with his hands up, or I'll cut you in half."

Slowly, Carter got to his feet, his eyes glued to the man's white knuckle resting on the trigger.

He opened his mouth. He was about to shout at Kim, not to bring him in but to warn him, when a soft voice came from the rocks to his right. "Hello there, mate."

The Aussie submachine gun chattered. Slugs stitched up Sin Chai's body from his belt to his head. The better part of it sprayed from the man's shoulders as if it were being forced through some macabre shredding machine.

By this time, Carter had sunk back to his knees. He heard Kim, and then felt the man's hands under his armpits, lifting.

"God, man, they did work you over."

Carter managed to get his breath. "Yeah, but it looks a lot worse than it is. How did you know?"

"I phoned your talkie in to Rangoon. They had a return message with a Double Red designation. I was headed toward the hotel to find some way to get it to you, when you came through the window and all hell broke loose. All I had was my pop gun. Couldn't take four with that, so when they poured you into the car, I followed."

"You're a good man. C'mon, let's use their car."

"You still want to go for Chong's place?"

"More than ever," Carter replied. "We'll just change the plan a little."

At the car, Kim got it running while Carter took the bag apart. He strapped on his Luger and assembled the M-16. When he had the spare ammo belt around his hips, he climbed into the passenger seat.

"By the way, what did Rangoon have that rated a Double Red?"

"A woman's body was found on Santa Isabel Island in the Solomons last night. It was identified this afternoon as one of our people."

Carter's jaw clenched and his face drained of color. "Jillian Sorbonnia . . . they found her."

"Looks that way. She was pretty badly tortured before she died."

"Chong will pay for that," Carter hissed. "Let's go!"

Now he knew how they had gotten on to him.

FIFTEEN

They drove on by the road leading out to Chong's peninsula-perched mansion, and abandoned the car a half mile south. There they cut over to the coast and made their way on foot back over the cliffs.

In a rocky pocket, Carter dropped to his belly and scanned the ocean below the cliff. The boats were there. They showed no running lights, but there were guide lights on the pallets as the crane lowered them full from the mansion to the sea and brought them back up empty.

"They're working," Carter murmured.

"I can see," Kim replied. "But I think we have only one choice . . . take them or the house."

"I think you're right," Carter agreed, nodding. "Let's hope Rangoon has an intercept. You take the front, I'll take the back."

He hooked two of the incendiary grenades on his belt from Kim's personal armory, and took off. In seconds they were separated by rain and darkness. Carter made his way along the cliffs and then down toward the sea. The boats were loading less than thirty yards from the face of the cliff

161

and the steps cut into the stone up to the mansion.

He expected a sentry to be posted in the rocks near the sea both north and south of the loading area.

He wasn't disappointed.

On this side of the cliff, a wall ran to the edge of the sheer rock face above Carter. There was no way it could be scaled from his position, even if he had the equipment.

Staying near the cliff face, he moved forward in spurts, listening for any sign other than the steady rain from above or the crashing sea at his side.

Then Carter saw him. The sentry stood under an overhang, trying to keep himself dry from the rain and the spray of the surf. He stood motionless, holding a machine pistol by the stock with the barrel pointed toward the ground.

Carter paused in the depths of a wall indentation several feet from where the sentry stood. Carter screwed a silencer onto the barrel of the Luger and reholstered it. He tensed his right forearm and felt the hilt of the stiletto slide into his palm.

If he missed with one, the man would die with the other.

He moved stealthily along the base of the cliff, any sound he might inadvertently make smothered by the pounding surf.

He was less than five feet from the man when his presence was sensed. When the sentry whirled, Carter lunged. He brought the long barrel and silencer of the Luger down across the man's skull, and when he fell forward it was onto the razor-sharp blade of the stiletto.

He died instantly, and Carter eased him to the ground. He wasted no time, but moved on. Closer in now, he could see that the boats were using lights but the bulbs were blued, not recognizable from a distance.

It looked as though three of the smaller ones had already been loaded. They were laying farther offshore, waiting while the two larger ones were being loaded.

That was good, Carter thought. It meant they would be headed toward the rendezvous with the freighter as a flotilla, and, as such, would be easier for the speedboat from Rangoon that awaited them to follow.

Carter waited until the crane from above had lowered a flat almost to the deck of the boat and the men were busy guiding it before he moved. He darted over the rocks, staying as much as possible in the shadows until he reached the spot he had gone up earlier.

Without pausing, he made the first plateau, and as much by feel as sight found the rough-hewn steps.

He was halfway up, when he heard footsteps coming down. There was no place to go. He had sheer rock to his left and a fifty-foot drop to the ocean and rocks on his right.

He fell on his belly, the silenced Luger before him in both hands. The footsteps grew louder, and then he saw the glow of a cigarette in a cupped hand.

He waited.

Twenty feet. Ten feet. At five feet, he fired twice, catching the man dead center in the chest. Before he hit the steps, Carter had holstered the Luger and caught him. He hoisted him in a fireman's carry and went on up. At the path around the foundation of the house, he unceremoniously dumped him and continued on.

The outside door in the wall gaped open. Carter moved through it into the inner courtyard.

The inner door was locked.

He pressed his ear to the door. Nothing, no sound came from the other side. Evidently, Johnny Po figured that only exterior sentries were needed.

Carter pulled a piece of flexible wire from his ammo belt and inserted the curved tip into the keyhole. He worked it skillfully until the rusted tumblers clicked free. The entire operation took less than ten seconds.

He gripped the knob, gave it a twist, and pushed slightly as the door swung inward on reluctant hinges. He stepped inside and used the slender piece of wire to relock the door.

If the sentry he had left on the path were discovered, the locked door would slow them up a little.

He was in a dungeon-like room, small, cramped. It smelled like a barnyard after a rainstorm. An adjoining room held rack after rack of wine. He guessed correctly. It was right under the kitchen. Seconds later, he found the stairs and went up. A door at the top opened into a small sleeping area.

In the corner of the room, pushed against the wall, was a rickety twin bed, its frame covered by a wafer-thin mattress scored with rips and tears.

On the mattress was a frail old Chinese woman. Her eyes opened wide when she sensed Carter's presence above her.

"Don't call out, old woman," he growled, making sure she saw the silenced Luger. "I mean you no harm. Do you understand?"

She nodded fearfully and crossed her arms over her breasts.

"Do you speak Mandarin?"

"Yes," she managed, fear clogging her throat.

"The girl, May Won, she is here?"

"No. Her brother came for her hours ago. The old man is dying."

Carter nodded in satisfaction. "How many men on the roof?"

She shook her head and shrugged. Carter believed her.

"Are there back stairs to the third floor, to Chong's office?"

She hesitated. Carter dropped the barrel of the Luger until it nestled behind her ear.

"I said I didn't want to hurt you, old woman. I didn't say I wouldn't."

"There," she said, pointing a gnarled finger. "The kitchen. There are stairs to the third-floor hallway."

While she spoke, Carter slipped an ampule from his belt and broke off its tip. He jammed the hypodermic into her hip right through the sheet that covered her.

"Don't fight it," he said. "It is only to make you sleep."

She didn't even hear the last word before the drug enveloped her. Carter went into the kitchen, found the door, and mounted the narrow, dark stairs by feel.

Cautiously he cracked the third-floor door. The hallway was empty, illuminated by a small-watt bulb. Above, on the roof, the labor of the crane could be heard distinctly.

He moved across the hall to Chong's office. The door was locked, but again the wire easily removed the obstacle. Inside, he locked the door behind him and, with the aid of a penlight, went to work.

Swiftly but methodically he searched the room: closets, tables, desk, bookcases, under the carpet, behind pictures.

Nothing.

Carter was positive that, because of Johnny Po and the heavy artillery guarding the mansion, as opposed to Chong's digs in Rangoon, any records that existed would be kept here.

Angry at himself, he went back over the room again, moving more slowly this time.

He was about finished, cursing in frustration, when his elbow happened to jiggle a shelf on the back bar. The liquid in all the bottles rolled from side to side. The liquid in a large bottle of seltzer didn't move. Carter shook it, and still it didn't move.

He didn't bother trying to find the key. He smashed it.

It was all plastic, down to an inner case. And inside the

case was a roll of papers. Quickly, he looked at the contents.

Names, dates, places, bits of microfilm. It was blackmail material on every important person in the Burmese government.

Carter whistled low.

This was the reason Sydney Chong could operate so blatantly in such a closed society. He owned the men who controlled the society.

Carter slipped the papers into his belt, under his shirt, and checked the hall. It was still empty and the noise was still going strong from above.

Quickly, he ran down the hall and threw open the front window. He flashed his penlight twice, and immediately got two flashes in return.

That meant that Kim had already taken out the two gate guards and he had the rockets in place.

Carter flashed once more, a "go," and darted through a door to his right. He left the door open a good eight inches, and jacked a shell into the M-16, flipping off the safety.

From the doorway he had a clean sweep of the stairwell.

The first blast came about thirty seconds later. The rocket hit somewhere on the inner wing of the fourth floor. At once there was wild confusion above him, and Carter set himself.

He heard the whine of the second rocket, a delay, and then there was a jarring explosion directly above him.

That one did it. There was the sound of pounding feet in the upper hall and then they were coming down the stairs. There were eight of them massed and jammed together.

Carter waited until they were halfway to his landing, and then opened up with the M-16. He sprayed from side to side and worked his way up. A couple of them returned fire, but their confusion made the shots go wild, mostly through the open hallway window.

Four were dead on the landing. Two were dying on the stairs, and two were wounded, trying to make their way back up as they returned fire.

Carter couldn't make Johnny Po in this bunch, but that was to be expected.

That snake wouldn't be one to panic and run so quickly unless he knew where he was running to.

Carter jammed a new clip into the M-16 and bolted for the stairs. One of the two wounded had life enough to struggle his machine pistol into a firing position.

Carter sprayed both of them and went on up. He unlimbered one of the grenades. Outside, he could hear firing from the Aussie submachine gun. Either Johnny Po had men on the first floor, or some of the men from the boats had decided to check out the racket.

There was silence above him now as Carter knee-walked up the final flight of stairs.

He couldn't smell smoke and he saw no flames. If Kim's rockets had started a fire, it had been extinguished by Chong's men or the rain.

Carter poured a burst into the upper hallway and followed it. He had barely hit the deck and rolled when a door to his right opened and two slugs thudded into the wall behind him.

He kept rolling toward an enormous sheet-covered couch. At the same time, he sprayed the ceiling until the small bulb lighting the hallway shattered.

He came up to the far side of the couch and heaved. It took all the strength in his legs and shoulders to push the behemoth of mahogany and upholstery away from the wall. At last it moved, and he fell behind it, ramming yet another clip into the M-16.

None too soon.

The first shooter was still trying to pop him, while a door on the opposite side had opened and a hail of slugs was now coming his way from there as well.

Cross fire.

He didn't dare use the grenade: the space was too confined. The resulting fire would probably reach him from the incendiary before it got to them.

He flung himself to the far side of the couch, leaned out quickly, and got off two shots, one to each door. He ducked back as the cross fire came at him again, but he had made them cautious enough to be wild.

He raised up behind the couch, getting off two more quick shots. He had to get them away from the doors, even at the risk of drawing their fire.

And then, over the blast of return fire, he heard it: the sound of the crane. Either Johnny Po was taking a powder, or he was bringing up reinforcements via one of the pallets.

Outside, Carter could hear a full-scale battle being fought between Kim and the men on the boats. It was only a matter of time before Chong's people figured out that there were only two people in the invading army. When that happened, they would use their numbers and all hell would break loose.

Carter couldn't stay stuck behind a couch in the hallway any longer. If he could gain the opposite wall, he could cut off at least one main line of sight. He got off a burst around the couch and rammed home a new clip as he moved.

A bullet tore through the back of the couch just as he leaped for the opposite wall. He wheeled, the M-16 at his hip barking. The slugs shredded the door and it wobbled open. The man behind it was doing some leaping himself, trying to lose himself in the sheet-shrouded furniture.

Just above where he was crawling, Carter spotted a huge, heavy mirror. He aimed carefully and put a burst into the mirror.

It worked.

The mirror shattered, spraying the room's occupant with shards of glass. He came up cursing, his clothes shredded and his face oozing blood. As his eyes searched wildly for Carter, the Killmaster fired again. The slugs stitched across his chest in a perfect pattern, and he slammed into what was left of the mirror, leaving a bloody streak on the wall as he slipped down.

Now for Johnny Po and his sidekick in the crane room. Carter could still hear the winch and cables bringing the pallet up.

He leaned out from the wall, took a look, and ducked back. Twice he did this and drew no fire.

Slowly he moved along the wall.

The door was closed and the sound of the crane had stopped.

Carter was tensing himself, when another door, farther down the hall, opened and two men rolled out firing. The Killmaster dropped to his belly and emptied the clip in their direction.

Bingo time. They both died without zeroing in on him.

Carter ran down the hall to the open door. The time for games was over. He pulled the pins on both incendiary grenades, counted, and heaved them into the room. He backed off to the first door and waited.

The explosives were less than a second apart, and Carter moved with them. He hit the door with his shoulder and rolled through. One man stood by the crane. Carter cut him down with his first burst. The M-16 clicked on empty. Carter reached for a new clip, and a foot came from the shadows behind him to kick the weapon out of his hands.

The body of Johnny Po followed his foot, and Carter felt as though a small building had fallen on him. He rolled with the weight, managing to draw the Luger. Po saw it and grabbed Carter's arm. He slammed the Killmaster's knuckles into the hardwood floor, and the Luger skittered away.

Carter came up with a hard left that caught the other man full on the ear. Po rolled away with a roar, and both men were on their feet, facing each other.

The situation wasn't good. Both grenades had spread their fire along the inside wall of the huge room. Large doors had been cut into the outer wall to bring the pallets through for loading. Over a hundred crates were stacked near those doors now, and it was only a matter of minutes before the fire reached them. When that happened, the whole top of the house would go and the lower floors would soon follow.

Add to that the problem of Carter's bruised and aching body against a man like Johnny Po, and things looked bleak.

Po was advancing, leering. "You bring me joy, man. I will kill you with my hands."

He threw a series of solid punches, but Carter managed to absorb most of them on his upper shoulders and arms.

Carter stepped away and came back with two quick lefts, the second snapping Po's head back. The big man seemed surprised, then angry, and he came in at Carter again, this time putting more weight behind his punches. He missed with all but two: one of them a grazing right to Carter's chin; the second more telling as it landed on his right side, sending almost shattering pain shooting up the arm, into the shoulder, and even halfway up the neck.

Carter knew he couldn't take many more of those, if any.

Po came at him again, and this time one of four punches landed, catching the Killmaster on the chin and sending him reeling backward. And Po came right after him. They closed, arms around each other's neck, feet grappling with one another, each of them trying to trip his opponent to bring him down.

It was a grunting, brawling stalemate, and Po was trying
to break it with his teeth. Twice he tried to get to Carter's
neck, to tear away at the jugular.

Carter felt the mouth clamp his shoulder, biting into his
skin. Po's knee came up, trying to smash into the Killmaster's groin. Carter blocked, but then the knee worked between his legs, levering him, twisting him clumsily to the
floor. Po landed on top, his forehead battering Carter's face,
a hand clamping over his throat.

Carter struck with his own left and saw a lip pulp. He
struck again, and found the bridge of Po's nose. The sharp
edge hammered again and again until the bridge splintered.

Still it wasn't enough and the vise around his throat was
closing.

Carter arched in pain, trying to throw his opponent off,
but the stocky body rode him like a jockey, each extremity
fighting, tearing.

Again, Carter went for the nose with the heel of his hand,
trying to find the proper angle that would drive the splintered
bone up into Po's brain.

It was impossible.

The room was filling with smoke now. Carter could see
the fire, fed by furniture, inching closer and closer to the
munitions. If the stalemate didn't break soon, they would
both buy the farm.

And then Po himself, through his own impatience, created
the break Carter needed.

He released Carter's right arm so he could use both hands
on the Killmaster's neck.

In that split second, Carter threw his arm out straight and
tensed the muscles in his forearm. The spring-release in
Hugo's chamois sheath responded instantly, and he felt the
friendly hilt caress his palm.

Carter brought the deadly blade up from behind, worked

it beneath Po's ribs, and pushed in the blade with all his strength.

He heard Po gasp for breath. The head began a convulsive, sudden thrashing from side to side. The mouth gaped open, but no sound emerged.

Carter twisted the blade and dug it in deeper.

From Po's throat came a sudden ghoulish rattle, and then nothing.

Carter pushed the body away and watched it sprawl, lifeless, to the floor. He struggled to his knees and then to his feet. Through dazed eyes he found Wilhelmina and staggered to the opening.

The three small boats had taken flight. Carter could see them moving out into the center of the bay. Below him, he could see one of the larger craft ablaze. Evidently, Kim had managed to lob a couple of the incendiary grenades onto it from the shore. The second boat was moving, trying to maneuver, but Kim, from the shore, was making it hard. He was laying down a constant line of fire across the deck and the wheelhouse every time a head or body popped up.

There was no time to use the crane and pallet. The fire was already licking at the crates.

Carter moved to the very edge, took a deep breath, and jumped. He hit the water with his toes pointed, and slid under smoothly. But when he came up it was on the starboard side of the boat, away from Kim's covering fire, and he had been spotted.

Using the superstructure to shield them from Kim's slugs, two men were sighting in on Carter with their rifles.

But just as they were about to fire, the flames from above did their job.

There were three small explosions, and flames burst from the wide opening where Carter had just jumped.

And then the big one went off. The entire fourth floor of the mansion went skyward and the third became kindling.

The two shooters were distracted, and Carter dived. He swam underwater to the boat, surfaced, and began to move around the stern.

He couldn't pinpoint Kim, but he found the man's general area from the bursts of fire.

The house was an inferno now, and above him on the ship, it was chaos. Suddenly, over the noise, he heard a shout.

"Get out, get out! There!"

It was Kim, and he pointed out "there" by firing a burst into a tree about seventy yards to Carter's left.

The Killmaster dived and swam about a third of the way before surfacing. As he gulped air, he chanced a quick look behind him, and saw why Kim had urged him to get out. Fiery debris from the house had fallen on the big boat's decks. Flames were licking fore and aft, and it was only a matter of time before the boat went the way of the house.

Carter dived again and urged his weary body to respond. Two more trips to the surface took him in among the rocks. He was just pulling himself from the water when the boat went. A huge ball of orange rolled into the sky. Combined with the already burning mansion, night had been turned into day. Carter sprawled out on a rock and let exhaustion take him.

It could have been minutes or hours later when he felt friendly hands turning him over and he looked up into Kim's grinning face.

"You are a one-man demolition force."

Carter managed a half smile. "I almost became a cinder myself."

"Po?"

"He's in there," Carter replied, nodding toward the mansion.

"Good. What next?"

"Do we have any transportation?"

"Hell, yes, the big man's limo. It's down by the gate. The metal may be a little hot, but it's drivable."

"Then let's go. We'll pick up May Won and Zeke and head for Rangoon."

"Chong?"

"Yeah," Carter said tightly, gaining his feet, "Chong."

"You sure you can make it?"

"I'll make it," the Killmaster growled, striding toward the car.

SIXTEEN

Carter sat in the back of the limo, sipping from a bottle he had found in Chong's mobile bar. The big car was parked in an alley bordering the center-city bazaar. He had been sitting there for fifteen minutes while Kim took Zeke and May Won into a nearby house where they could hide from Sydney Chong's people until it was over.

He saw Kim move out of the shadows and walk toward the car. His face was grim.

"Well?" Carter asked.

"Bad news. Francine and Chong never showed at the restaurant."

The Killmaster nodded. "Figures. Once he got on to me, he probably figured she was in up to her eyeballs as well. Did the blackmail files work?"

"Oh, yeah," Kim said. "All the big shots are very relieved. They've already sent two boats after the freighter. It will be turned around and ordered back into port."

Carter sighed and sipped. "Chong won't know about that or Kamwaddy yet. That will be our surprise.

"You don't want the government here to handle it?"

"No way," Carter replied. "Even with his power base

gone, Chong has enough financial clout to buy himself out. He'll just get out of Burma and set up shop somewhere else."

"Then we go?"

"Yeah, we go," Carter said. "With the layout of his Rangoon estate we got from May Won, it should be a cinch getting in. And once we're in, surprise is on our side."

"What about Francine Camway?"

"Chong won't have touched her yet. Me, he could just kill and dispose of the body. But he knows that she's legit. He'll have to plan some 'unfortunate accident' for her."

"When do we go?"

Carter checked his watch. "Now. It's five in the morning," he growled. "Best killing time there is in the world."

As Kim started the engine and pulled away from the curb, Carter lifted Sydney Chong's skeet gun from the floorboard and started shoving in shells.

Chong's estate was about a twenty-minute drive outside Rangoon. They parked about a mile away and moved through a grove of trees until they could get a good look-see.

The grounds were huge, surrounded by a chain link fence made less severe in appearance with plantings of ornamental shrubs, vines, and trees. There were two roads leading in and out, both with security guards in small huts just inside the gates. In front of the gates, Carter could see speed breaks to keep vehicles from approaching too quickly.

"Would you say Mr. Chong was security conscious?" he asked dryly.

"I'd say that, yes," Kim chuckled. "Let's check out the rear."

They moved to their left on through the trees until they came up along the river. There was no fence, of course, but Carter located tiny trip wires in crisscross patterns along the ground and leading down into the water. One step on any one of them and an alarm system would go off instantly.

"It's like a mine field," Kim hissed. "We can't walk through it and we can't swim ashore without setting something off."

"Yeah," Carter said, frowning as he studied the layout further. Then he remembered the boathouse and small marina they had passed about two miles upriver. "C'mon, I think I know how we can get in."

They returned to the limo and drove back up the winding river lane to the boathouse. Other than a couple of small night lights, it was dark and there was no one around.

Carter picked the lock on the door and scavenged until he found everything he needed.

"A harpoon gun?" Kim asked, wide-eyed.

"Yeah," Carter said with a grin. "And an antique at that. It works by catapult pressure, like a bow and arrow. Nice and powerful, nice and silent."

He swung a five-hundred-foot coil of thin but strong nylon line over his shoulder, and led Kim down to the pier.

There was a small, beat-up inboard speedboat and two larger sailboats. Carter chose the one with the tallest mast and went aboard.

"Cast off the lines."

Kim did as he was told and jumped aboard, grinning. "I think I get your drift."

They used the little outboard for half the distance, then killed it. Kim used an oar, gondola style, to keep them steady in the current while Carter rigged the line and the harpoon gun.

"Okay, cut in here!" Carter suddenly hissed.

Skillfully, Kim swung the bow over, and the current did the rest. When Carter was satisfied with the position, he dropped the stern anchor, then waited until the bow came around and secured it the same way.

He waited until the slack was out of both anchor lines

and the boat was riding steady before he set up the gun.

"Okay," he said, "watch the line and don't let it drop."

"Which tree are you going to use?"

"That big one near the fence on the right."

"What happens if you miss and hit the fence?"

"Then get ready to dive over and swim in!"

Carter set up the gun and aimed for the very top of the densely limbed tree. When he was sure the trajectory was right, he nodded to Kim. He got a return nod, crouched behind the gun, and fired.

The powerful, silent springs sent the harpoon high into the air, with the nylon line sailing behind it like the vapor trail from a jet.

"Be there, baby," Carter urged.

It was. The harpoon sailed through the leaves with a hissing sound, and Kim yanked the line.

"It's caught, solid."

"Good," Carter said. "Up you go!"

Kim went up the mast. In seconds he had wrapped the line around a sail cleat and dropped it back down to Carter. The Killmaster attached it to a hand winch and turned the crank until the line was taut and the boat was listing slightly from the pull.

"Ready?" Kim asked.

"Go ahead," Carter said, and went up the mast himself.

Hand over hand, the two men moved along the line . . . twenty, forty, fifty, sixty feet.

"Now!" Carter hissed, and they both released to drop to the ground.

For just a second, they both tensed as they hit.

There was no alarm.

"So far, so good," Carter growled. "Let's go!"

The cement walk was a bright, light stripe in the moonlight as it led past ornamental hedges, flower beds, and a gazebo.

It went through a long, dark arbor covered with vines, then the backyard opened onto a tennis court and a wide expanse of flagstone around a swimming pool.

Carter knelt in the shadows at the end of the arbor, looking at the house. A long row of sliding glass doors and picture windows on the right side of the house were dark. Lights were on in two rooms upstairs, and in the kitchen on the left side of the house.

Kim pointed to the two lighted windows. "According to May Won," he whispered, "that's the room where they'll probably be holding Francine."

Carter nodded. "When we hit the house, you keep going around the side to the front. Get in that dense shrubbery. When all hell breaks loose, make sure you get those two gate guards before they can get to the house."

"You going in?"

"Yeah, through the patio door. Let's go."

Carter crouched and ran past the tennis court, his shoes scuffing softly on the cement. Kim was a silent shadow as he darted along beside him. They slid to a stop in the shadow of the small cabana by the swimming pool, and looked around again.

Nothing. No one. Silence.

They took off again. At the corner of the house, Kim kept going. Carter moved across the patio into the shadows by the rear door.

Very slowly, he tried the door. It was locked. There was a faint click as he picked the mechanism. Quickly, he stepped back into the shadows, listening, his ears attuned to any sound of movement beyond the door. When he heard none, he pushed the door inward silently, closing it gently behind him, unslinging the shotgun from his shoulder.

Quickly, he passed through the patio room and listened again. There was no sound in the darkened house, except for the muted whine of the air conditioning.

He moved down the hall and through the swinging doors of the kitchen.

The light he had seen through the kitchen window had been small, dim. Carter had mistaken it for a night light. Instead, it was the light from an open refrigerator, and standing there was a man.

He turned as Carter came through the door. Incomprehension registered on his face just long enough for Carter to move and gain the upper hand.

In two steps, the Killmaster was on him, smashing a rigid forearm into his neck, breaking it like a rotted plank. He rocketed across the room to a table, fell to his knees, rolled over on his side in slow motion, and lay still.

Again Carter waited, his body tense for any reaction to the sound of the man's body crashing into the table.

When there was none, he moved into the lower hallway of the house. A wide stairway led up to the second floor. Cautiously, he climbed and then checked up and down the hallway.

Light shown under two doors.

He checked the first. It was locked. The knob of the second turned. He left it alone and lightly rapped with one knuckle.

A guttural voice full of sleep answered from the other side. Carter growled something indistinguishable in the same singsong pattern of the other's language, and stepped to the side.

He heard the tread of bare feet, and raised the M-16. The door opened. The man got no more than his head and shoulders into the hall when Carter brought the barrel of the M-16 down with all the strength in his shoulders and arms.

The man's forehead struck the door with a loud thump. He slid down it onto his knees, a revolver falling from his limp fingers. But he didn't go all the way down.

Carter kicked the revolver away and slugged him with the M-16 again, harder this time. The man moaned and toppled sideways heavily. But he didn't look all the way out even yet; his skull was exceptionally thick.

When he tried to raise himself one more time, Carter used the sharp side of his hand on the back of his neck.

That ended it.

The Killmaster dragged him by the legs into the room and locked the door.

It was a bedroom, and empty, but there was an open connecting door to another bedroom. Through it, Carter could see Francine Camway on the bed. Her wrists and ankles had been tied to the four bedposts.

Her eyes were closed, but he could detect the steady rise and fall of her chest.

Quietly, he crossed to her side and placed a hand over her mouth. Her eyes popped open at once.

"Miss Camway, I presume?" he whispered, and lifted his hand.

"My hero," she replied tartly. "Untie these bloody things!"

When the last tie came loose, she sat up with a suppressed groan, rubbing circulation back into her arms and legs. Carter checked the places where the ties had bitten into her flesh and pronounced her fit. She looked up at him.

"Kamwaddy?" She asked it as if she'd already guessed the answer.

"Done," he replied. "Po's dead. Is Chong here?"

"Yes," she said. "He drove from Kamwaddy directly here. Then two of his bloody goons tied me up."

She got off the bed gingerly and tried to stand. She fell against Carter, grabbing his shoulders for support. He put one arm around her and held her up.

"Take it easy, wait until you get the blood flowing again."

He went on to explain about Hong Kong, Macao, and the agent from Manila, Jillian Sorbonnia.

"You mean, Chong killed her?"

"Had her killed," Carter replied, "and tortured her first." His lips set in a tight line. "She was a tough cookie, and would have held out as long as possible. But Chong's men are animals, ruthless. When she couldn't hold out any longer, she probably gave his people a description of me, and when it matched, Chong put two and two together."

"Bastards," Francine hissed, and took a few steps.

"All right?"

She nodded. "What now?"

"Chong," Carter said. "Any idea where his quarters are?"

"He came in here a couple of times to ask me questions. When he left, he always turned that way," she replied, nodding down the hall. "His bedroom is probably in that wing of the house. What are you going to do?"

Carter held an ampule up to her eyes. "He's going to have a very serious heart attack."

Francine shuddered, but Carter could tell from her eyes that she accepted it. "And after?"

"Kim gets us out of the country very quietly. Tonight's business here, and in Kamwaddy, will be quietly covered up by certain people in the government."

He retrieved the revolver from the guard's body in the other bedroom, and returned, handing it to her.

"You stay here. Lock the door behind me. If anyone other than Kim or myself tries to get in, use this."

He didn't wait for a reply. In the hall, he waited for the lock to click and then moved on.

At the opposite end of the hall, he ran into huge double doors. This, he guessed, would be Sydney Chong's suite.

He was about to reach for the knob, when suddenly he

heard the sound of a car pulling up in front of the house. He darted to a window just in time to see it stop and May Won jump out.

"Shit," he hissed, and darted back down the hall and into another room.

Luckily, the room was empty. Through a crack in the door he saw May Won run up the stairs and bolt for the double doors. She left one of them open behind her, and Carter heard voices.

He moved into the hall and slipped to the open door. He was about to roll into the room, when the voices got louder. May Won screamed. There was a thud, and Carter made out Sydney Chong's angry voice.

"You little fool! You think you could kill me?"

Carter peered through the crack. May Won was sprawled on the floor, the side of her face already turning blue. Chong, in elaborate silk pajamas, was just bending over to pick up a small automatic.

She *was* a fool, Carter thought. She must have gotten away from Kim's people and decided to exact her own revenge.

Carter set the shotgun aside. In close quarters like these, the scatter-gun wouldn't discriminate. If he had to fire, the girl would probably catch some of it.

He drew Wilhelmina and stepped into the room. "Just lean over and put it on the floor, Chong."

The man's face registered veiled surprise. "Why, Mr. Ellison . . . or whatever your real name is . . . how ever did you get out of Kamwaddy?"

"By limousine," Carter replied evenly. "Your watchdog, Johnny Po, is dead, and your act is over."

A thin smile played across Chong's face. "I don't suppose you're for sale . . . ?"

Suddenly, two things happened at once. May Won made a leap for the gun in Chong's hand, and all hell broke loose in front of the house.

Kim had been spotted and drawn fire.

The combination drew Carter's attention for a split second. It was long enough.

Chong used the girl's leverage and threw her into Carter. The automatic fell to the floor, but Chong let it go.

Instead, he followed the girl, his feet windmilling. He was as fast as a cobra. One heel caught Carter full in the face. The other foot slammed his arm against the door. Wilhelmina spun from his grasp and he had his hands full with Chong's follow-up attack.

A vein in the middle of Chong's forehead was standing out now, throbbing. He kicked again at Carter, catching him in the gut. Carter buckled and fell to the floor. Chong came in to finish him, a foot aiming at the Killmaster's head, a murderous grin on his face.

He moved forward and launched his body into the air horizontally, his right leg bent almost double. At precisely the proper time, he straightened his leg viciously.

But the death-dealing kick never landed.

Carter rolled to his back and scissored his own leg up. He kicked upward just as Chong released. The other man's blow hit Carter's shoulder just as the Killmaster's foot slammed into Chong's groin.

A hideous shriek of pain emptied from his throat and he fell to the floor, holding himself.

Carter sank to the floor himself. It was almost over. He brushed the perspiration from his face and out of his eyes. When they were clear, he looked around for the Luger. When he spotted it, he leaned forward.

"No . . . not yet."

He looked up.

May Won was standing beside Chong, the little automatic held steady in her hand.

Carter started to rise.

"Don't move," she said.

Behind her, Carter saw Kim appear in the doorway. He raised the Aussie submachine gun and glanced at Carter.

Slowly, the Killmaster shook his head and Kim lowered the gun.

May Won looked down at Chong writhing in pain on the floor. Something wild had come into her eyes. Her mouth twisted savagely.

She aimed the gun carefully and squeezed the trigger. It made a soft snapping noise. The slug went into Chong's body, very low. A bubbling scream came out of his wide-open mouth and his body heaved halfway up off the floor.

She shot him again, in the same place. He settled back down on the floor with a high-pitched whine, the brutal face contorted in agony. Froth trickled from one corner of his mouth and both hands clutched weakly at the blood pouring from his groin.

May Won stood over him, watching his agony avidly. She went on watching until he was dead. Then her face became cold and a film seemed to form over her eyes. She dropped the gun on Chong's inert, bloody body, and turned to face Carter.

"My family is at peace," she said calmly.

Carter could only nod. Maybe, he thought, it was better this way. He rolled his eyes to Kim.

"Get her in the car."

Carter holstered his Luger, and on leaden feet walked down the hall.

"It's me," he said, rapping on the door.

It opened at once. Carter took the revolver from Francine's hand, wiped it free of prints, and dropped it onto the floor.

"It's over. Let's go."

"Where?"

"Out of this damn country first . . . "

"And then," she said, wrapping an arm around his waist, "I know a little village, with a little cottage, and . . . a great big bed."

DON'T MISS THE NEXT NEW
NICK CARTER SPY THRILLER

CODE NAME COBRA

Carter paid the bill and, when she returned, excused himself to go to the men's room.

Guillermo was already there, washing his hands. The male attendant paid them little attention. He was far too young and far too healthy for the job. He was one of Orbán's troops. The attendant in the ladies' room across the hall was also a plant.

"Well?" Carter murmured, scrubbing his hands under the tap in case someone came in.

"She used the phone in the ladies' twice. The first time, there was no answer."

"And the second?"

"A woman. It was jibber-jabber. Actually, it sounded

like a drop number. Knight asked if she could have a fitting tomorrow. The other woman said two o'clock would be fine."

"Did you get the location?" Carter asked.

Guillermo nodded. "It's a dress shop by the university on the Calle de Sans. It's owned by an Italian woman named Caprezzi."

Carter dried his hands and studied his own frown of concentration in the mirror. "It doesn't sound like part of a Cobra operation."

"Not at all," Guillermo agreed. "Maybe we're going up the wrong tree?"

"Maybe," Carter said. "But right now it's all we've got. Everything set?"

"Just hit the switch when you make your U-turn at the end of the street. We'll be on you the minute your windshield shatters."

Carter nodded and moved to the door. "Just make sure your boys aim wide."

Guillermo smiled. "They're all sharpshooters, don't worry."

When Carter got back to the table, Sabrina was sulking. "You certainly took a long time."

"Sorry," Carter said, taking her arm and leading her toward the exit. "Must be all that wine."

She smiled, working a breast against his bicep. "It's all right. I had the same problem."

He handed her into the car, walked around, and slid into the driver's seat. He started the engine and drove slowly toward the cul-de-sac. He was halfway through the U-turn when he reached under the dash and flipped a toggle switch.

There was a muffled explosion, and the windshield shattered before them as the planted explosive squib went off.

Carter cursed and Sabrina screamed, burying her face in her arms.

The Killmaster swerved and the right front fender smashed into a wall. The car had barely halted when the passenger door was yanked open. Sabrina screamed again as powerful hands yanked her from the car.

Carter was already rolling out his own side, Wilhelmina in both hands. Without pausing in his movement, he threw himself, belly-down, across the hood.

Guillermo and another man had Sabrina a foot off the ground, and one of them was trying to cover her face with a towel. Carter could smell the chloroform from where he was. It was obvious from the fear in Sabrina's face that she, too, could smell it. Fear, yes, but she was fighting back . . . kicking, biting, gouging, and scratching with everything she had.

Carter fired. The blank in the Luger was a number ten load. It sounded like a Howitzer in the confines between the buildings.

The second man howled with pain and the front of his white shirt erupted red. He staggered back and fell. Sabrina tried to twist away, but Guillermo got an arm around her neck and pulled her in front of him as a shield.

Carter launched his body off the hood of the car and hit them both. The three of them went down, with Sabrina rolling free. Guillermo came up firing. Carter waited. Two slugs blew out the side windows of the car.

If that doesn't convince her, he thought, *nothing will.*

He tried to chop the gun out of Guillermo's hand, and lost his own in the process. Guillermo stepped in for the hand-to-hand, and they went at it. Carter hoped it didn't look too much like a rehearsed ballet.

He brought his right foot crashing down on the arch of

Guillermo's foot. As the other man's body jerked with pain, Carter smashed at the gun and threw himself to the right at the same time. He heard the shot and the bullet whistling harmlessly into the night sky.

As the gun went off, Carter chopped with the edge of his hand. Guillermo staggered. Carter measured and swung his knee. The Spaniard turned just in time to take the blow on his inner thigh, but he howled in pain and hit the pavement grabbing his crotch.

"Nick, there are two more of them!"

Carter grabbed Wilhelmina and whirled. Two more of Orbán's men were racing toward them from the open end of the street.

"C'mon, run!"

"My heel," she cried, "it's broken!"

"Kick your shoes off and run!"

She did, like an antelope, with her fingers in Carter's belt and footsteps pounding behind them.

"It's a dead end!" she shrieked.

"Not if we go over that wall," Carter said.

Before she knew it, he had his hands under her butt and she was on her way to the top of the wall. She had the presence of mind to grab and haul herself the rest of the way up. The Killmaster quickly followed. Just as they were both going over, two slugs screamed off the bricks not more than three feet to their right.

Jesus, men, Carter thought, *you don't have to be too authentic!*

He dropped first and half-caught her. He grabbed her wrist, and they took off down a narrow street.

"This way!" he yelled, when they hit a larger street.

"I . . . can't . . . my chest . . ."

"You've got to. They'll be coming around the block any second!"

She fell and skidded. Carter simply yanked her unceremoniously back to her feet and they were running again.

Two blocks farther on, they came out of the dark street onto a wide boulevard with lights, people and cars.

"Nick . . ." Sabrina gasped from behind him, "I . . . can't . . . run anymore . . ."

"You don't have to. There's a cab." He pushed her into the back seat and barked the address of the hotel to the driver.

"Sí, señor," the man said, his broad, mustachioed face beaming in a smile.

It was Orbán's driver.

Carter leaned back and lit a cigarette. He wasn't surprised when he saw his hands shaking. He proferred the pack, but Sabrina shook her head, her eyes to the front.

Carter took a deep drag on the cigarette and managed to keep a straight face all the way to the hotel. He paid the driver, whispered, "Wait," and caught up with Sabrina at the door.

Walking at her side through the lobby, he checked her out of the corner of his eye. Her face was pasty and she seemed physically ill. She approached the elevator unsteadily, wobbling on her bruised feet.

"You all right?"

"I'm as good as dead," she hissed dully. "Just as good as dead."

The elevator came down and the door opened. By the time they reached her floor, she was crying softly, the mascara running down her cheeks in wavy lines.

Orbán's men were still in the hallway. She went through them without even seeing them, and, inside, headed immediately for the mini-bar. Still shaking, she twisted the cap from a miniature, downed it, and attacked another.

"The bloody bastard tried to kill me . . . *me!*"

The façade was gone now. Whoever and whatever she

was, Carter thought, she was not an old pro who had been under fire before.

He moved forward and put his hands on her shoulders. "I'm sorry. I thought he might try something like this, but not so soon."

She whirled. "You set me up!"

He shrugged and tried a lopsided smile. "You said you wanted to help."

"Bastard! You bloody bastard!" she shrieked.

Her hand whipped around faster than Carter could catch it, and his head rang from the slap.

"Out! Get out!" she screamed. "I don't want to see you ever again!"

Carter backpedaled. "The guards are in the hall. You're safe now . . ."

"*Out,* you son of a bitch!"

She threw the miniature and it shattered on the door just as Carter closed it.

He paused by the guard at the elevator. "You know what to do."

The man nodded. "Let her go anywhere and do anything. Just act like we're guarding her."

"That's it," Carter said, and stepped into the elevator.

In the cab, he whistled all the way to Orbán's office.

—From CODE NAME COBRA
A new Nick Carter Spy Thriller
From Jove in September 1988

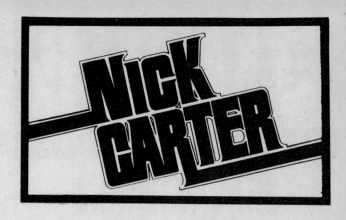